I0788202

the obsidian curse

The Lunaterra Chronicles

l. penelope

Cover design by Bookin' It Designs

Page edge design by Painted Wings Publishing Services

Copyediting by Sydnee Thompson

Heartspell Media, LLC

ISBN: 978-1-944744-35-9 (eBook)

ISBN: 978-1-944744-36-6 (Paperback)

ISBN: 978-1-944744-37-3 (Hardcover)

THE OBSIDIAN CURSE

L. PENELOPE

also by l. penelope

the bliss wars series

Savage City

Beastly Kingdom

Brutal Fortress

earthsinger chronicles

Song of Blood & Stone

Breath of Dust & Dawn

Whispers of Shadow & Flame

Hush of Storm & Sorrow

Cry of Metal & Bone

Echoes of Ash & Tears

Requiem of Silence

the eternal flame series

Angelborn

Angelfall

other romance

The Cupid Guild Complete Collection

writing as leslye penelope

The Monsters We Defy

Daughter of the Merciful Deep

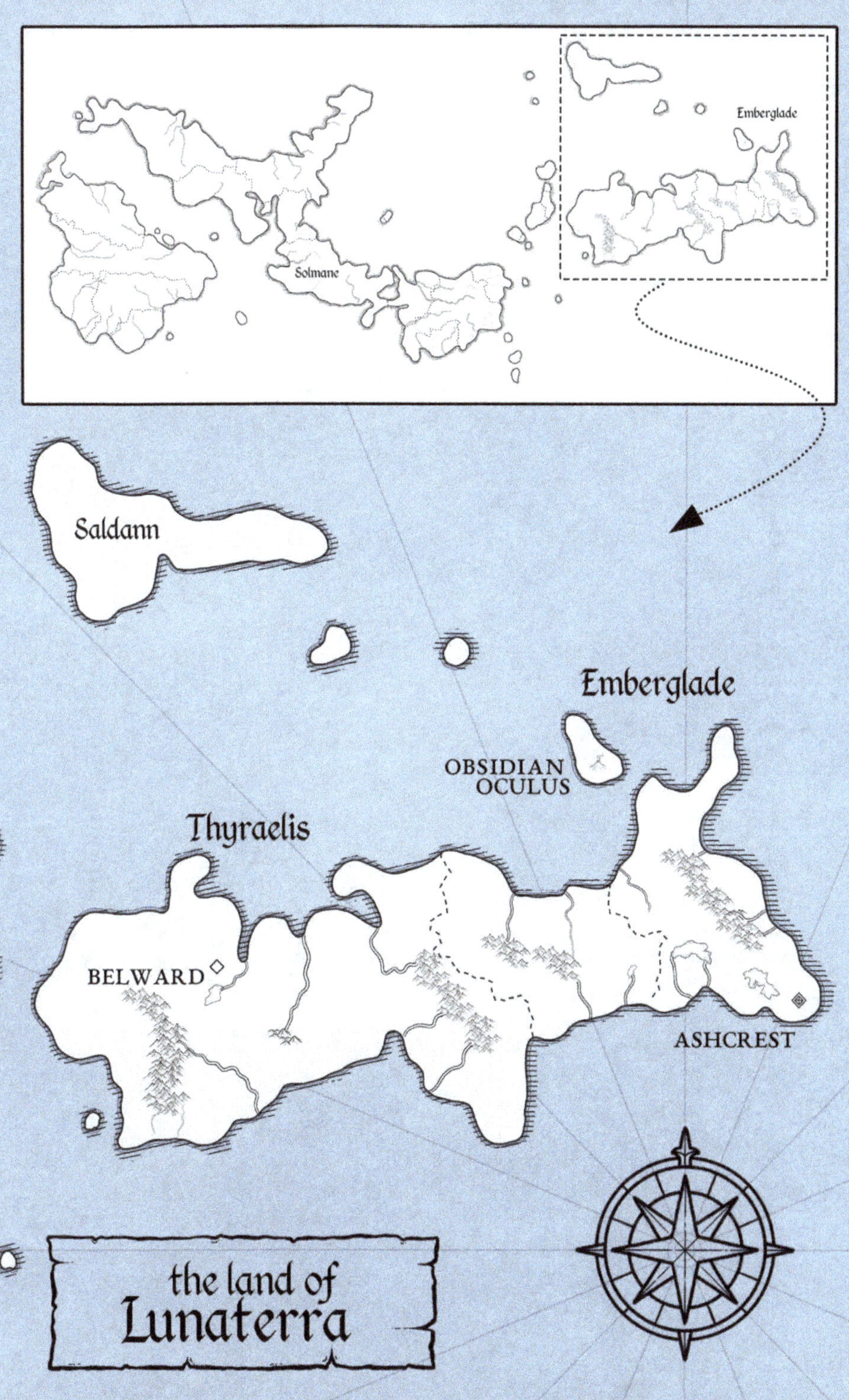

Emberglade
Solmane
Saldann
Emberglade
OBSIDIAN
OCULUS
Thyraelis
BELWARD
ASHCREST
the land of
Lunaterra

1

niara

THE RITUAL CHALICE shook in my hands, its contents sloshing alarmingly as I raced up the steep and rocky incline. I could neither afford to waste a drop nor could I slow my pace. Nerves made my breaths come too quickly. That, plus the altitude, was making me lightheaded.

To my right, the twin suns nearly embraced as they sparkled over the Aurelian Sea, but the sheer drop from the mountain path to the water stole much of my enjoyment of the view. The packed earth of the trail was soft and crumbled with my every step. My foot slipped, and a shower of pebbles cascaded over the side, making my heart stop.

I paused for a moment to catch my breath, but I didn't have time to waste. I could not be late.

The delicate crystal chalice, inlaid with precious multi-colored seaglass gemstones, was a vital element of the Day One ceremony. If anything happened to it, or if it didn't make it into High Priestess Valya's hands before the dual eclipse began . . . I couldn't even contemplate the consequences. All the forbearance the High Priestess had shown me thus far would certainly dissolve, and then where would I be?

I hugged my body closer to the mountain, willing my nerves to settle and my hands to stop shaking. Tradition dictated that the chalice be carried half full of waters from the Aurelian to the Obsidian Oculus, the sacred site of the Day One ritual. I had been given this auspicious task, and I could not afford another failure.

Rounding the final bend before the cavern's entrance, I was ready to breathe a sigh of relief when the light was blocked by two tall figures stepping in my path. The man and woman both wore dark armor inlaid with gold etchings that seemed to absorb all light. The man's skin was a deep copper, while the woman's was closer to my own dark ochre. But both of them had hair that was the red-gold of a newly lit flame. Ember Fae.

"May the flow be upon you," I said, bowing my head in greeting. I'd only rarely ever seen an Ember Fae before, though they ruled the land of Emberglade. I'd been born and raised in Tidehaven, a Water Mage city. However, the Obsidian Oculus was not only sacred to us; the Fae also held the site dear. More than one war had been fought over access and rights to what to outsiders was little more than a cave inside an active volcano.

However, seventy-five solars ago, a peace accord had been struck. Given that Water Mage and Ember Fae holy days did not coincide, we now shared the Oculus, albeit with guards from both races stationed around the clock to maintain the peace. Usually, the Fae soldiers stayed out of sight, so I'd never had any interaction with them before. When the two did not move from my path, I looked up, a question in my gaze.

"We must search your bag," the female Fae said, her voice brooking no opposition.

I clenched my teeth, trying to hold back the instant annoyance springing up within me like a geyser. "That is not a part of the Oculus Accords." There. That was perfectly polite and mannerly. More like the gentle stream I was meant to be embodying.

The male Fae answered in a deeply resonant voice. "The Accords state that in the event of a breach by one party, such methods may be taken by the other party to redress that breach." His tone made goosebumps rise on my arms regardless of the warmth of the day.

"What breach has occurred?"

His mouth snapped shut. The woman glanced over at him. That's when I noticed the twin markings on their foreheads. They wore no helmets, but the brightness of their hair had distracted me. Along their hairlines lay identical, intertwining curved lines. They were a mated pair.

My eyes widened as they appeared to speak to each other without uttering a word. As far as I knew, Ember Fae were not telepathic, but as a child, I'd read stories about them. Fairy tales that told of fated mates bonded by something called *twining*—a magical merging of spirits.

Water Mages had no such custom. My parents had a very happy marriage from what I could tell, and part of me was glad they'd died together so they were never separated, but it was still a far cry from a spirit bond that meant a mated pair found it painful, deadly even, to be physically distant from one another for too long.

Finally, the woman spoke up. "An important ancient text has been stolen from our archives in Ashcrest. We have been ordered to search all, human or Fae, who enter any of the holy sites."

My ire cooled, and I turned to expose the satchel slung across my body. "Feel free to search it." I lifted the chalice slightly to show I did not have my hands free.

The woman nodded solemnly and bent to rifle through my bag. I resisted the urge to tap my foot impatiently. The mother and daughter suns were nearly in alignment. My satchel contained very little, as I had few possessions. Acolytes in the Order of Morros didn't exactly take a vow of poverty, but we also didn't earn an income and so had little coin with which to accumulate material items.

Of course, I was no longer an acolyte. The reminder was a jagged shard slicing my skin. I winced, and the female soldier glanced up at me sharply.

Finally, finding nothing, she stepped back, and the Fae allowed me to pass. I speed walked the rest of the way and entered the mouth of the cavern with almost no time to spare.

2

niara

TWO WARDENS STOOD GUARDING the inner entrance of the cavern. As I passed, I nodded at them politely, holding the chalice even more reverently in my hands.

"Lovely of you to join us, Niara," an acerbic voice called out from my right. Ylena—make that Priestess Ylena, as she demanded I refer to her—stood in all her ceremonial regalia. Like the other priestesses, she wore a dress of ice blue embedded with crystals. A headdress studded with seaglass gems ranging from blue to purple to green topped her dark hair.

I banked the fires of jealousy that licked at me and ignored her, making my way carefully across the slick floor —made of the volcanic glass which gave the Obsidian Oculus its name—to the altar where High Priestess Valya waited.

Overhead, the domed ceiling was interrupted by a perfectly smooth hole opening to the heavens. Directly below it lay the sacred pool full of glittering dark water. The pathway surrounding it was wide, and the altar lay directly across from the cave's entry. I spared a glance upward to check the position of the suns.

"Filling the Day One chalice is quite a responsibility for a Tidemaiden," Ylena said, hounding my steps.

"It is standard for the First Tidemaiden," I replied, taking the bait, then groaned internally. I should have kept my mouth shut.

"Oh, yes, of course, *First Tidemaiden*, how could I have forgotten that? Perhaps you being the *only* Tidemaiden is why it slipped my mind. Wasn't it kind of the High Priestess to throw you that bone? Had I been her, with an acolyte who failed her trials five times in a row, I wonder if I would have been as magnanimous."

Her words were blades delivering cut after cut. Ylena and I had never been friends. But when we'd started out together as initiates to the Order, we'd at least been friendly. Now, her greatest pleasure in life seemed to be tearing me down.

"How grateful we are, then, that you are not the High Priestess." I imagined her face drawing taut with anger but didn't bother to turn around to see.

I moved as quickly as I dared across the glassy ground, not as scared as I once was to step on the ancient script that covered every surface. As an acolyte, I'd been entranced by the swirling, looping collection of characters perhaps crafted by Morros's very hand. Apparently, neither the Ember Fae nor the Water Mages had ever been able to translate the writing, so its meaning remained a mystery. I'd even heard a lecture from the High Curator theorizing that the text may actually predate the arrival of the first humans to populate the planet of Lunaterra, my long distant ancestors who were pilgrims from some distant world.

Stepping foot in this sacred place always made me feel connected to history, to my legacy, to the reasons I wanted to join the Order in the first place. Even in the face of my failure, I could not shake the deep feeling of importance that being here elicited.

I had finally reached the altar, where Valya stood serenely. She inclined her head to me before carefully taking the chalice from my hands.

"Thank you, Niara." Her voice was the gentle lapping of waves on the shore, embodying the peace of the Eternal Flow.

Our High Priestess was the most powerful Water Mage in Emberglade. As a child, before being sent to the Order's care home, I had assumed that she and the other Archons who led our people would be old and withered. Instead, she was in her late thirties with smooth, unlined skin the color of freshly tilled soil and a manner so tranquil my shoulders dropped several inches every time I was in her vicinity.

We were both orphans, but she had moved from initiate to acolyte to priestess in record time, passing each trial on the first go. Her water sculptures were so beautiful they regularly brought grown men to tears. She'd mastered all five specializations, had undergone warden training as well, and held several competition titles in the martial art of Fluidhand. She was the ideal of Mages and everyday Flowfolk alike—everything I wanted to be, but was so far from achieving.

The overhead lighting changed subtly, indicating the beginning of the eclipse. I had made it by a hair. Fortunately, this meant that Ylena had duties to attend to aside from pestering me.

During celestial events, such as the weeklong series of eclipses of our planet's two suns and thirteen moons that was about to begin—the Holy Convergence—light from above would illuminate the etchings on the walls, giving them a magical glow in purples and blues. I was as excited to see it as I was for every other part of this rare event.

The Day One ritual that was about to take place represented the unity of the Water Mages with our patron moon Morros, the Melancholic Guardian who tempered the fiery exuberance of the world with his calm wisdom.

Two men approached the altar, causing me to step back. High Curator Danir was the stereotypical aged scholar, white-haired with a tangled white beard and eyes clouded with age. High Warden Amal, however, was even younger than the High Priestess, with sand-colored skin and eyes of glittering onyx that always held a smile.

His gaze snagged mine, and he winked, causing the blood to heat in my veins. The leader of the Mage defenses, he was from a wealthy and powerful family. As such, he was sought after by women throughout the land. Why he persisted in singling me out, complimenting me, and giving me small gifts was still a mystery. Just that morning, I'd found a delicately carved figurine of a rose, crafted from magefrost, in my mail cubby. I couldn't help the smile that came to my lips remembering it.

The ceremony was beginning, and the gathered priests, priestesses, and acolytes each held their chalices before them, simpler versions of the grand chalice that Valya used. Using the seaglass gems that allowed Mages to channel Morros's power, one by one they conjured streams of water from the sacred pool, causing them to rise and enter their vessels.

The writing on the walls was beginning to glow as the suns came into alignment. Just as the combined voices of the chant to begin the ritual rose, the ground beneath our feet rumbled. I was knocked sideways and crashed hard into the wall, bruising my back and hip. The chamber shook wildly, dust and gravel falling down upon our heads.

The once placid waters of the sacred pool bubbled and frothed as if heated from below. Screams rang out, and the wardens rushed forward, forming a barrier between the water and the rest of us, conjuring magefrost spears and shields as they went.

From the water, fire began to lick up toward the oculus overhead. Steam filled the cavern. The heat grew more intense. The water rippled, and something began emerging from its depths. I peered around the legs of the wardens blocking me, more entranced than afraid of what was happening.

Out of the flames dancing across the surface of the water, two horns appeared. Then came an enormous dark head, maw open, bellowing out a roar that made my blood chill.

A colossal beast made of lava and fire arose screaming from the waters. It was at least the height of two men, with a thick chest and wickedly large arms. Flaming wings flapped on its back, blowing scalding air into our faces. Glowing red eyes surveyed the scene and did not appear to like what they saw.

The wardens blasted the creature with pressure streams of water and projectiles of magefrost. The monster howled in pain. Part of me had feared our weapons would be no match for it, but just as in the mundane world, water and fire did not mix.

The beast retaliated, conjuring a flame whip and lashing out at the wardens. Fire met ice with sizzling blows, turning the air almost too steamy to see through. A warden went flying across the cavern, crashing into the wall several feet away.

The air cleared somewhat, and I got a better look at the creature as it spun this way and that, parrying the attacks of the dozen wardens gathered. Amal was in the lead, a fierce expression on his handsome face as he battled the beast.

When another warden fell to the monster's fire whip, I caught the creature's eye. It was little more than a flaming pit inside a face of hardened lava, but it captivated me. Was it my imagination, or was there intelligence within? And though I knew it must only be in my mind, I could swear the beast was looking at me as well.

I should have been terrified, cowering in fear like the others, but what I really felt was curiosity. The sense that this creature was more than it appeared.

Suddenly, the monster stopped its thrashing and gave another ear-splitting roar. High Priestess Valya struggled to her feet and leaned on the altar. She gripped the egg-sized seaglass gem she wore on a pendant around her neck and began to conjure. A bubble of water emerged from the pool, large enough to enclose the creature, and snapped in place around it.

The monster thrashed and struggled and fought but was unable to free itself from the water cage. The enormous sphere floated from the center of the pool to the side, settling on the obsidian path. High Warden Amal produced an enchanted seaglass collar, one surprisingly large enough to fit around the creature's massive neck, and cinched it into place.

As those around me slowly recovered from the terror and shock of the past minutes, I worked to catch my breath. That moment my gaze had collided with the beast was seared into my mind like a brand.

3

niara

"THOSE EMBER FAE demons have much to answer for," Amal growled. "Setting this monstrosity upon us during our Holy Week." His hands tightened into fists and he glared at the creature in question, which sat motionless in the water cage near the entrance to the cavern.

"So you believe this to have been perpetrated by the Fae?" Valya asked, her elaborate headdress tinkling. The Day One Ceremony had been completed, albeit more rushed than I'd ever seen it. Afterward, the three Archons gathered in conference to discuss what to do. As was custom, the rest of us, all the priests, priestesses, wardens, curators, and me, sat around the pool as witnesses to their deliberation.

"Who else could be behind this?" Amal responded. "Nothing like this has ever happened at the Oculus before. The Fae guards stopped all our people as they entered the cavern. Perhaps their true purpose was to plant some kind of summoning device or work some other infernal mischief upon us in order to attack in this way."

"That would spit in the face of the Accords," High Curator Danir said, mouth contorted in outrage. "It would be tantamount to a declaration of war."

"Do you put it past them?" Amal spat. "It is only through Morros's blessing that we have a fighting chance against them at all."

The enmity between the Water Mages and Ember Fae was many hundreds of solars old, starting when they invaded this land that our ancestors had called home for generations. The peace accords, struck before any of us were born, were still considered new, and many deeply mistrusted them.

Valya stroked the smooth surface of her seaglass pendant the way she always did when pondering a big decision. "The question remains, what do we do with it?

"It's clear this creature is very powerful. We do not know how many wardens would be needed to subdue it. My magic is keeping it in place, but only because I'm channeling Morros's power constantly in order to do so. It is a strain that cannot be kept up indefinitely." She did not sound strained at all, but that was why she was High Priestess.

"The strength of this beast is immense," she continued. "We cannot simply keep it caged forever."

"Quite true, quite true," Danir responded, stroking his long beard. "After the Holy Convergence, we can scour the archives to determine if such a creature has been encountered before."

Amal shook his head. "With all due respect, High Curator, more research will not protect us. This thing is an abomination. It could have killed all of us today. A dozen of the best wardens we have could barely scratch it. I believe that we should take it along with us to the royal wedding in Solmane and bring it to the Convergence Games, where the strongest warriors on all of Lunaterra will be gathered to compete. The combined might and magic of those gathered would certainly be enough to destroy this terror. Will you be able to maintain the cage while completing the rest of the Holy Week rituals?"

Valya looked thoughtful and nodded. "Yes, I believe so. That is a novel idea, High Warden. I think we should bring this to the assembly." She waved her hand to those of us seated around the pool, listening in.

"Accusing the Ember Fae of setting this creature upon us would definitely breach the peace, something that we are certainly not ready to do," she said. "So our options are to cage the beast until more research into its origins can be completed or transport it to Solmane's tournament, where it can be destroyed. What say you? Priestess Larai, I should like your thoughts."

One by one, High Priestess Valya went around the circle, asking those gathered their opinions. Many agreed with High Warden Amal that the best idea would be to take the monster to the tournament to be defeated in the games. The curators all agreed with their leader. Then again, more research and study tended to be their answer for everything.

Once everyone had been asked, I expected Valya to take it back to the Archons for the final vote. However, instead she turned to me.

"And you, Niara, what do you think?"

My skin tingled uncomfortably as all eyes were cast my way. "M-me?" I stammered.

"Yes, dear. In conference, all opinions are heard."

Valya's kindness warmed me, so I girded myself to answer. "Well . . . I . . . I'm not entirely sure why we can't just put it back where it came from."

Snickers sounded around the circle. Ylena stared at me like I'd suggested eating babies for dinner. Amal's lips curved into a smile.

"Your tender heart does you credit, Niara," he said. "But we cannot allow this *thing* to exist and potentially threaten others at this sacred site."

He turned back to the Archons. "The majority of those assembled are in agreement with the tournament plan. What say you?"

High Curator Danir tugged on his beard and nodded. Valya hummed for a moment before also giving her assent.

"All right," Amal said. "Then what we must do is distract those two Ember Fae guards out front. If they did somehow plant this beast, we do not want them to know our plans. We must move the creature to the flotilla in secret and start our journey before nightfall."

The ancient rules of the Holy Convergence meant that we could neither travel on land nor sleep on water during this ceremonial week. The Order's flotilla was already prepared to take us west toward the nation of Solmane so that the three Archons might pay their respects at their royal wedding celebration in two weeks' time. Their tournament was just before the wedding, and the fact that both aligned with the Holy Convergence was fortuitous. As the First Tide-maiden, I had been excited for weeks to take this journey, my first outside of Emberglade. But now, with a captive in tow? I wasn't so certain.

I glanced again at the creature, currently subdued in its water cage. It sat in a disturbingly human position, knees up, arms around them, head bowed. The glowing embers beneath its thick hide of lava were dim. It looked like it was asleep.

Still, an impossible thought clung inside my mind. Something deep within me was certain that the beast's attention was even then focused on me.

4

niara

THE HOLY CONVERGENCE flotilla was made up of thirteen vessels, one for each moon of Lunaterra. The High Priestess's ship, *Morros's Tear*, a yacht named after our patron moon, sailed in the center of the others. Surrounding her were the other Archons' vessels: High Curator Danir's schooner with its graceful bridges connecting the library, art gallery, and infirmary on board, and High Warden Amal's galleon, with its hull of reinforced steelcrystal, six feet thick and impenetrable. Surrounding them were the barges belonging to the Order, skiffs for the lower curators, and the maneuverable, highly armed cutters for the wardens.

When the flotilla set off in late afternoon, there were only a few hours of travel remaining in the day. The mother sun had already set and the daughter sun was heading to her rest.

Though we eventually needed to travel west, we instead sailed to the northeastern corner of Emberglade in order to dock for the evening. The locations for each day of the Holy Convergence were very specific. Each eclipse was only visible in certain places, and so we followed a path set out by the heavens instead of the most efficient route.

The Day Two ceremony would require a new robe for the High Priestess, and I busied myself packing her overnight bag as the ships prepared to set anchor for the evening. Once her tent had been raised on the sandy shoreline, I began preparing her quarters, laying out her night things, and inspecting every item she would need for the next day's ritual.

Though these were my duties, my intense focus on them was not simply due to a desire to make sure everything was perfect. I was doing everything I could to drown out the sense of the creature's presence.

The High Priestess's tent was in the center of camp, while the beast was being kept at the edge, barely within reach of the magelight globes that cast an aquamarine glow over everything. With my every move, I was aware of its presence, even though it was not within my field of vision.

I decided to sleep under the moons and enjoy the clear, warm night. As the First Tidemaiden, I was essentially a glorified lady's maid. However, the ceremonial responsibilities put me closer to an acolyte than a servant. The reality of being too much of one but not enough of the other meant I did not really belong with either group.

My best friend Safina, a warden, had offered to save a bunk in her quarters, but aside from her and Amal, I didn't much like spending time around the wardens. There was a pallet I could use in Valya's tent, but I knew how much she valued her privacy and how little alone time she got. There was a space for me in the cooking staff's lodgings... but the outdoors called to me.

Morros would not be visible for several days yet, but even still, I hoped the fresh air would do me good. My bones were weary when I finally lay down to sleep, praying that my dreams would be restful.

SWEAT BEADED ON MY SKIN, providing the tiniest bit of relief from the unrelenting heat. I opened my eyes to find the sky above me was red and featureless, unbroken by any celestial objects—not even so much as a cloud.

I sat up to find myself wearing a scrap of umber brown fabric that barely covered me and lying upon a desolate field of black. My palm skimmed the strange surface that looked rough and felt smooth—it was not unpleasant to the touch.

The warmth in the air moved from oppressive to gentle and calming as my skin absorbed it. I was like a sponge for heat, craving more and more.

Though I was decidedly alone and the only thing alive as far as the eye could see, a voice rumbled in my ear, deep and rich. It caused a shiver to ripple across my skin, speaking words in an unknown language. Though the words were foreign, the tone was oddly . . . enticing.

The voice sparked a deeper heat within me, causing me

to squirm where I sat. A compulsion, impossible to ignore, had me skating my fingers across my chest, just under my collarbone, and then lower. Brushing over the tips of my nipples, which hardened at the contact. Down between the valley of my breasts to my belly and lower. To the space between my thighs that had begun pulsating with need.

I whimpered, squeezing my legs together, seeking some kind of friction to relieve the ache. All the while, the voice brushed over me in waves, a soft scrape against my sensitive skin.

From the collection of strange sounds, words I understood began to coalesce.

"Does that feel good?" The silken, thunderous sound caressed my ear. There was no one nearby, no one for this voice to belong to. Still, part of me wanted to live inside of it.

The vibrations rippled across me, through me, penetrating my skin until I could feel them inside of me, all the way to my tender core. Moments later, my fingers followed, brushing against the tight curls on my mound and finally plunging inside my center, stroking wetly as the voice urged me on.

"Like that, touch yourself just like that. Stroke yourself with those clever fingers. Make yourself feel good."

Pleasure within me burned, consuming all other sensations. I chased the building inferno that was unleashing itself within me.

The voice's encouragement pushed me, made me want to please it, knowing that my ecstasy would also satisfy it. I strummed my fingers inside me, against my delicate bud, until I burst.

Endless lightning bolts of pure bliss sizzled through my

body, seizing my limbs and making me cry out. I sobbed until the delicious tendrils of the peak faded, leaving me once more on the ground.

The voice quieted, and I was left panting with heat searing me from the inside out.

5

niara

I HELD my breath throughout the entire Day Two ritual as the priests and priestesses created elaborate water sculptures under the eclipses of the moons Sylvos and Ryxis. Each man and woman puppeted their creation with masterful control, portraying the story of Morros bringing life to our ancestors—magical beings who shifted into creatures of the sea. Though after many generations of intermarrying with humans, Water Mages no longer boasted these transformational abilities and required seaglass gems in order to channel magic, we still honored those distant forebears several times a solar.

While I'd always loved watching aquasculpture displays —probably since it was the one I'd most wanted to master, and failed the worst at, of the five specializations—the restless sleep of the night before had taken its toll. I struggled to hold back yawns throughout the entire ceremony.

The dreams I'd had were so vivid. And unusual. My cheeks simmered recalling them, and though I knew it was unlikely that anyone was paying me any mind, even thinking about last night around others was making me self-conscious.

Could it have been Amal's flirtatious glances that had sparked such charged fantasies? Or had the loneliness just seeped too far into my soul? I couldn't remember ever having dreams like that before and wasn't sure if I wanted more or not.

Sweat broke out along my hairline, and I recognized the lie in my thoughts. I *did* want more, and not just in dreams but in real life. As a girl, I would stay up late into the night, long after lights out at the care home, reading stories of the Fae and their twining. I would yearn for someone who would want to be close to me like that . . . someone I would never be separated from.

My best friend Safina would scoff at the notion of such forced closeness. "Don't they tire of being around each other all the time?" she'd ask. But I never thought so. It seemed so romantic to me.

I had been alone for such a long time. Amal's appreciative smile from earlier in the day came to mind, and I sighed. He was everything that any Water Mage woman could want: handsome, kind, talented, powerful, rich. Could he truly be the *more* I wished for?

Regardless of my swirling thoughts, I managed to carry out my duties without a hitch and even earned an approving nod from High Priestess Valya.

That night, I chose to sleep under the stars again and was plagued by a similar dream of heat cascading across my body. I woke with Sylvos high in the sky above me, the greenish tinge of the Forest Moon especially intense. There was a pulse, a sixth sense deep within me, beating louder and louder. I could *feel* the beast in its cage across the camp, and that awareness was growing stronger.

Unsure if I would be able to get any more sleep that night, I rose, intending to head toward the sea. Since I was a girl, I'd found the sight and sound of waves lapping against the sand calming. When I decided to join the Order—or attempt to, anyway—I would often take refuge at the seashore and pray that the tranquil waters would help to mold me in the proper shape of one of Morros's children: serene, patient, and wise.

However, instead of moving toward the water, my footsteps led me in the other direction, across the sand to where the beach gave way to high, coarse shrubbery. To the outer edge of the camp where the water cage lay.

The wardens were on their rounds and none had been stationed to guard the prisoner, trusting in the magic of the cage. The magelight here was dim, its faint echo glinting off the thin barrier of water that protected the rest of us from this creature of lava and flame.

Inside, the beast sat just as it had at the Oculus. The bubble of water was not tall enough for the monster to stand and not wide enough for it to lie down outstretched. It sat, knees bent, arms resting on them, head down, as I approached.

The broad back with its thick, black hide rose and fell with the creature's breaths. This close, the skin appeared to be made of stone. Jutting out of the area near its shoulder blade was a magefrost spear tip. The moment I noticed it, a sense of pain washed over me. Not my pain, the creature's.

I had accidentally cut myself with a magefrost spear once during self-defense training, and it was a fiery pain unlike any other. To have one lodged inside of you . . . The beast was already subdued, the enchanted collar around its neck no doubt holding a docility spell. Was there any reason to torture it further with this wound?

I looked around to ensure I was alone—I had no qualms about what I intended, but explaining would be difficult. Then I eased my arm through the water cage. I could reach in easily and be able to retract my arm—though if I entered it fully, I would be stuck.

The jagged shard of magefrost was, of course, cold to the touch. I plucked it from the creature's shoulder and dropped it onto the sand, where it melted with a sizzle. Strange. It must have had some extra enchantment on it. Normally, the magic would have held its form.

The beast didn't move. Though I should have been grateful it didn't react with a roar, or by trying to bite my arm off, I was a little disappointed.

I was just pulling my arm out of the sphere when a voice sounded in my head. A familiar voice. *Thank you*, it rumbled. *That was very painful.*

I stumbled back in shock and tripped over my feet, falling onto the sand.

keeran

Though I cannot see her behind me, the sound of her falling makes me wince. I did not intend to scare her.

Slowly, she gets to her feet and approaches my enclosure once more, walking around until she's within my eyesight. I need very little light by which to see, so the distant glow of magelight dancing across her face and caressing her high cheekbones is enough to make out her smooth, dark skin and full lips.

The night dress she wears clings to her curves, and the outline of full breasts and wide hips makes something within me, the part that is man and not beast, grow taut with anticipation and desire. I leash the eagerness that rushes up within me. My natural impetuousness will not serve me here. I must tread carefully.

Her gaze is wide with shock, but the fear seems to have dissipated, which pleases me. She casts a furtive glance around, ensuring we are alone, and steps closer to the cage.

"You can speak?" she whispers. Wonder fills her voice, and I drink in the sound, committing it to memory.

Directly into her mind, I say, *Only this way. We are connected, you and I.*

Her eyes widen dramatically. "How is that possible?"

I cannot answer that question. Not yet. Instead, I slowly lift a hand, hoping the fear does not appear again, and point to the collar around my neck. *Will you remove this?*

She looks at it, then back at my face. I've cooled the flames within, and I wonder what she sees. A nightmare from the pits of the Underworld?

Slowly, the beautiful woman before me shakes her head. It was a lot to ask, but I saw no harm in trying.

From the south, footsteps approach. One of their guards on his rounds. *Someone's coming*, I tell the little Water Mage. *You had better go.*

She blinks rapidly, peering around, though the guard is still too far away to be seen. Then she gives me one more curious glance and darts away, feet light on the sand.

A minute later, the guard marches up and peers at me through the barrier of water. I open my eyes, bringing the fire into them I'd banked for the young woman, looking every inch the terrifying beast they tried to kill. The man jerks back, pungent fear wafting from him.

I should have asked her name.

I have listened carefully for it, but even my elevated senses have not managed to catch it. But I am confident that her curiosity will spark again, and she will seek me out.

I look forward to that very much.

6

niara

I TRIPPED three times racing away from the beast's cage, the echo of its voice still reverberating in my mind. It wasn't possible, was it? This savage creature that had emerged out of the volcano and whom we had subdued could speak telepathically? Nothing about this made sense.

I needed to find someone I could talk to. I wasn't certain of the wardens' schedules, but I raced to the bunk Safina had pointed out to me and peeked my head in the doorway. Several women slept soundly on their pallets, but my best friend's, covered by one of the two poorly crocheted blankets we'd made as teens that she took on every assignment, was empty. I turned to leave and bumped into a taller figure entering the tent.

Safina was wrapped in a bathing sheet, having just come from the bathhouse. She grabbed my shoulders to halt my escape.

"You look like you've seen a ghost, Niara."

"I need to talk to you."

Whatever she saw in my face made her expression grow serious. "Two minutes," she said, and raced inside to dress. When she reemerged, she took me gently by the arm and marched me several feet away, where we couldn't be overheard.

"What happened?"

I told her about the dreams, of waking up and finding myself at the creature's cage, of removing the shard of magefrost from its back, and then of what it said to me.

As I spoke, nothing in her expression changed, but I knew her well enough to recognize the tiny signs of amazement and concern in the crinkling of her eyes.

"You're certain it wasn't some kind of trick?"

"What kind of trick would it be? And even if it was, if the creature is intelligent enough to trick me in this way, it's not the mindless monster that we should be carting off to the tournament to be killed." My breathing was fast and my heart rate elevated. "We should try to talk with it, parlay or something."

Safina pulled at the end of one of the thick cornrows her hair had been wrangled into and looked out into the distance. "You should take this to High Warden Amal. He will know what to do. They might even call a conference over it so that the Archons can discuss."

I nodded. "Yes, that makes sense. I don't want to burden High Priestess Valya, since she already has so much on her plate. I'll speak with Amal in the morning."

"He plans to sail with Valya tomorrow, anyway," Safina advised.

"Thank you for listening to me." I opened my arms, and she pulled me into an embrace.

"Always," she said. "We are sisters by choice, not by blood, and I will always be here to listen to you. If you would just go to warden training, we could serve together."

I pulled away and shook my head, then tugged the end of one of her braids. "Not having this discussion again. You know my Fluidhand skills are terrible, and I can't conjure a magefrost blade to save my life." Though she was a head taller and several stones heavier than me, our bond created as orphans was solid. It would have been nice to serve the Order together, but there was no area of magecraft that I hadn't failed terribly at.

I trudged back to my pallet behind Valya's tent and dragged it into the kitchen staff's quarters, not wanting to sleep alone that night. Then, I fell into a fitful sleep—without the erotically charged dreams I'd had before, but still hearing echoes of a powerful voice rumbling in my head.

THE RISING wind whipped my hair back, causing the beads at the ends of my many braids to tinkle. I lifted my head to the mother and daughter suns to feel their warmth on my skin as the ship pitched gently beneath my feet. The deck swayed in a lulling rhythm that was slowly becoming familiar to me. Breathing deeply of the salt-laden air, I willed calmness into my bones.

Day three was a travel day with no eclipse until the wee hours of the morning. The flotilla traveled at a sedate pace, slicing through the azure waters, the route mapped out carefully to ensure we would be in the visible range of each celestial event on the proper day.

Since breakfast, the Archons had been in private conference with one another, and I'd been patiently waiting. Shortly before lunch, Amal emerged from the High Priestess's cabin. I stood so swiftly from my place outside the door to greet him that my head swam. He grabbed my arm to steady me.

"Thank you," I said, basking a bit in the light of his gleaming smile.

"Niara." His voice glided over my skin. "I was hoping to catch up with you."

"Really? There's also something I need to speak with you about."

"Come." He led me down the steps below deck and over to a quiet nook with a portal window looking out into the waters of the sea. Once we were seated, I began my tale with no preamble.

I left out some details, such as the nature of the dreams and the fact that I removed the magefrost shard from the beast's shoulder, telling him instead that the creature spoke to me as I passed by on a late-night walk to clear my head.

Amal's brows furrowed as he listened. "You're saying the beast spoke to you in your mind?"

"Yes. And it was intelligent, almost cultured, like it had been educated. I don't think it's the feral creature that we've assumed. I believe we need to try to parlay with it. Perhaps it can tell us why I can hear it and others can't. Or maybe it's just that no one else has listened."

Amal drummed his fingers on his thickly muscled thigh,

gaze never leaving my face. "Thank you for bringing this to me, Niara. You've spoken to Valya already?"

I shook my head. "She's been so burdened by the extra pull of maintaining the cage and performing all the rituals. I didn't want to bother her with it. Since it's a security matter, I thought it best to bring it to you."

"Very wise." He moved his hand to pat my thigh in a comforting manner. "And compassionate of you. I must say, though, I think we should keep this between us for now."

"Really?"

His expression turned solemn. "You have one more acolyte trial remaining, is that correct?"

I dropped my head. An acolyte had only six times in which to undergo the trials to become a priest or priestess. After my fifth failure, Valya had installed me as the First Tidemaiden so that I could increase my skills over the solar revolution of service and attack the next test with more confidence. I had no idea if passing at this point was even possible; it seemed my magecraft grew worse and worse the more I tried. I had not totally given up on the dream, but it was near death.

Amal squeezed my thigh gently. "You cannot predict who will be a judge at the trials, and I would hate for anyone who hears of this unusual connection you have to the fire beast to have any cause for concern about you."

My shoulders tensed. I hadn't thought of it like that.

"For the sake of your future, I'm glad that you kept this with me. And I will keep your confidentiality. I hope you know I have the highest regard for you, Niara."

My cheeks heated. Under his hand, my thigh grew

warmer as well. "Why?" I couldn't help but asking. "I'm no one and nothing."

"That isn't true, Niara, and you know it. Your compassion is a credit to Morros. You are deeply loyal, effortlessly kind, and generous."

I wanted to add to his list the stream of complaints I usually heard about my personality—how my temper was too spirited, my anger unruly. I'd been working so hard on keeping these undesirable qualities under wraps, but they bubbled below the surface, never fully cleansed. It was part of the reason why my trials had failed.

"I have great admiration for you," Amal continued. "As I hope I have communicated. It is my most ardent hope that we can deepen our acquaintance." His hand slowly stroked my leg as he spoke. The sensation wasn't unpleasant, and a tremulous ache in my chest punctuated his movement. Dark eyes were fixed on me, a seductive quality to his gaze.

"I'm . . . incredibly flattered," I said, suddenly finding it hard to breathe. "But it's nearly luncheon, and I had better go and see to the High Priestess."

He nodded serenely and removed his hand from me. "Until we meet again."

I stood, trying not to appear flustered or like I was escaping. Instead, I effected a sedate pace as I retreated, his inviting expression lingering in my mind, my skin where he'd touched me through my skirt prickling with cold.

7

niara

THE FOURTH DAY of the Holy Convergence included only a half day of travel since the eclipse of the sun Lyra by the moon Aurelia would happen near noon. The ritual celebrating the patience and forbearance represented by Aurelia as he continually chased the daughter sun was also a brief one, though it required the most preparation.

The location of the ceremony where the eclipse would be visible was a rocky outcropping overlooking the Aurelian Sea. Getting to the overlook required an hour's hike uphill. My job was to carry the case bearing High Priestess Valya's ceremonial chalice, as well as the robe and headdress she would don. The headdress itself weighed nearly a stone, and the chest protecting it along with the chalice's container were bulky and difficult to manage on the walk.

We were halfway up the hill when I slipped on some slick stones, wet by a trickle of water flowing downhill, and landed hard on my knee. "Ouch!" I cried, only to hear a snicker. Ylena and another priestess were composing their faces, trying to hide their obvious mirth.

"Perhaps in your next prayer to Morros, you can request agility and grace," Ylena said, as the two picked their way around me.

I took a deep breath, tamping down the vexation building within me. *Don't respond. Don't respond.* The first tenet of the Order was to be like the water that shapes itself to any vessel. Even if priestesses like Ylena didn't embody the principles all the time, I could still try.

The geyser of emotion that threatened to burst from me began to die down. I steadied myself and rose painfully, looking down at the tear in my skirt. Blood was seeping through it from my knee. Fortunately, I could still bear weight on the leg, but it wouldn't make getting up the hill any easier.

Priests, priestesses, wardens, and curators streamed by me as I tried to find a better position for the cases I carried. Suddenly, the headdress chest was plucked from my grasp.

Safina was at my side and hefted the case easily, making it look as if it weighed nothing.

"Did you speak to Amal?" she asked.

"Yes, yesterday." I lowered my voice, though no one seemed to be paying attention. "He told me to keep the information to myself, that it wouldn't look good for me to have any sort of association with the fire beast, considering my history."

Safina's forehead crinkled. "Really? I don't see how anyone could blame you for this."

I shrugged. "I don't know, but he said he would look into it."

She hummed in response, still seeming a bit unsure. Her reaction made me think back to my conversation with Amal. Maybe I should have asked more questions.

We finally reached the top and Safina helped me take my burdens to the altar site, a large, flat stone near the cliff's edge. From this vantage, the view was breathtaking. The camp sprawled below, the tents being assembled by the staff who had remained behind. Beyond, the sand gave way to the turquoise waters of the Aurelian Sea, which stretched out, sparkling, to the horizon. The flotilla anchored nearby was majestic, an unquestionable display of Water Mage ingenuity.

Once Valya was dressed and prepared, I had little to do until the ceremony began. I sat near, but not too near, the cliff's edge, enjoying the calming sight of the sea glittering in the late morning sunlight. The breeze tugged at my skirt and cooled my heated skin. I wanted the rhythm of waves lapping against the shore to lull me into a state of relaxation, but it was slow in coming. The ache in my knees was a persistent drumbeat overpowering my attempts at calm.

It took me several minutes to realize that the spot I'd chosen gave me a perfect view of the beast's water cage. From this distance, I couldn't make out the features of any individual people—they all scurried like insects completing their duties. But the beast's black form inside the sphere of water was impossible to miss. Within the span of darkness making up its body, two pinpricks of orange flashed.

It was looking at me. Or rather, it was looking in this

direction, and that odd knowing inside of me was convinced that I was the focus of its attention.

You are in pain?

I jolted sharply at the voice in my head, jerking so violently I nearly fell over. My mouth flew open. I stared in shock at the small dot of black, which stood out in contrast to the pale sand.

"W-what?" I said aloud.

You are hurting, the creature responded.

"You can hear me?"

You do not need to speak aloud for me to hear you. As I said, we are connected. And I can feel you. Just as you can feel me. The voice was so low it was almost a growl, but the words were sure and direct. *Could* I feel the creature?

I focused, filtering through the emotions within me. I was in pain, my knee stinging and throbbing along with the rest of my muscles. Emotionally, I was spent, tired, confused, and a little afraid. However, I discovered a sense of calm within me that was not usually there. Also, a feeling of outrage, like day-old banked coals on the cusp of dying that could be easily revived.

How is this possible? This time I thought the question.

There is a great deal of magic in this world, it responded. *What is your name?*

Was there any harm in answering? Especially to a creature who could read my mind? *I'm Niara. Can you hear all of my thoughts?*

No, Niara. Only the ones you direct toward me. My name in its fathomless voice made my skin feel elastic across my body. This was a very intimate way of communicating, and I felt like I was doing something illicit. Like I should worry about being caught.

Do you *have a name?* I asked.

Not at the moment, the creature said, which I found a very strange reply. *Will you come and see me again tonight?*

I didn't know how to answer that. Such a thing was certainly a bad idea, and yet the pull to comply was strong. I was saved from answering by the ringing of the ceremonial chime. The Day Four ritual was beginning.

I rose and brushed off my skirt, attempting to push all thoughts of the beast from my mind as the moon slid into place, covering the daughter sun. But for the rest of the afternoon, I didn't feel quite so alone.

8

niara

I WAS DREAMING AGAIN. I found myself in that same land with the red sky overhead and the black earth beneath my feet. This time I was walking, and though pockets of steam geysered up from the ground every few feet and I could tell the place was searing hot, my bare feet were unscathed and the temperature did not bother me in the least.

I did not know my destination, but it soon became clear. A bed appeared before me in the middle of this vast wasteland. The thick mattress was covered in black sheets, and black flowing, gauzy curtains enclosed it. I approached and lay down on the most comfortable mattress I'd ever felt—it was like a pillow beneath my body, cradling me gently.

As soon as I settled, unseen hands ran over my exposed skin, beneath the slip of a dress I wore, until they tore it away from me, leaving me naked. Against the shell of my ear, warm breath from unseen lips whispered foreign words, their resonance a soft thunder that made my bones quietly vibrate.

Invisible hands ran up my legs, over my belly, skated across my breasts and up to my neck, my jaw. They caressed my skin reverently, raising my temperature and making my breathing grow shallow.

I spread my legs wider, an invitation. Every part of me wanted more of this feeling, wanted it to never end. The fingers stroked back down my body and dove between my thighs. I cried out and writhed, seeking to draw them in deeper, desperate for them to fill me.

They invaded me, stretching me and then curling, hitting a spot within me that I hadn't even realized was there. Whimpers of ecstasy escaped my lips as those thick fingers pumped in and out, massaging that pressure point that made me scream out involuntarily.

Sweat broke out across my skin. My entire focus was on the delicious intrusion of my body, on magnifying the pleasure being delivered. I reached for the unseen hand but felt nothing.

"Not yet," the voice told me. I whined at being denied. Then the speed and intensity of the hand's movements inside me increased. I could do little else but lie there and take the delicious onslaught.

A white-hot bolt of fire shot through me, starting at my core and radiating outward. A silent scream captured my throat as my body seized, pure bliss cascading through every muscle.

Afterward, my throat was raw, my limbs like jelly. Lungs

gasped for breath and the hands retreated. My eyelids shut, and I fell into a deep sleep.

WHEN I AWOKE, Morros was high in the sky, his brother moons distantly visible. Though it was late, I felt deeply rested. Maybe even restored.

The echoes of the dream vibrated through me. The passionate physical experience was also accompanied by a feeling of safety, a sense of acceptance. Perhaps it was just my imagination, but for a moment there, after reaching the peaks of ecstasy, I truly felt at peace.

I blinked, staring up at the Melancholic Guardian to whom the Water Mages owed so much, wondering what He wanted for me. Was peace at the end of this road I was traveling? Was my path truly laid out in His register? Was I walking in the direction He'd laid out?

Unable to stop my thoughts from spiraling, I rose and slipped quietly out of the tent so as not to wake any of the cooking staff. My feet whispered across the sand, my mind back in the dream. That voice whispering deep inside me. I was moving automatically, but my destination was inevitable.

He was waiting for me.

You're back, his voice growled in my head. So familiar— the voice from my dream. The beast in my mind.

A warden stood guard two dozen feet away on the other side of the cage, his back to me. He could not see me in the gloom, but he was still closer than I would have liked. I crouched, peering up at the creature, unable to make out any of his facial features in the dark.

How is this possible? I asked him mentally. *How are you in my mind and in my dreams?*

He opened his eyes, and those glowing embers trapped me in place. There was nothing human in them, but the intelligence there was impossible to ignore.

I cannot explain it, he replied, appearing to choose his words carefully.

Cannot or will not?

Those molten eyes pulsed with light, but he did not respond. Being this close to him was like a soothing balm across my skin. Cool water on a burn that eased an anxiety within me that I hadn't realized I'd held. I craved proximity to him.

It made no sense. This was a hulking creature of lava and fire. Terrifying in his size and power. Why was I drawn to him? Why could we hear each other's thoughts? Why did the thought of his touch launch a thousand butterflies within my chest? What was wrong with me?

My fingers brushed the surface of the water cage and I held myself back from piercing the barrier.

Will you remove my collar? the beast asked. *I vow that I will not harm you. I believe you know this to be true.*

Perhaps this was all an elaborate ruse, a trick, the creature using some arcane magic to lull me into a false sense of security with mental communication and passionate dreams. But I could sense his emotions deep within my chest. It was as if I had a second heart that represented him, and right now he was hopeful, cautious, pleased by my presence. There was nothing of duplicity there. Then again, what if this, too, was just a part of his power?

Will you harm anyone else? I asked.

Not unless they are trying to harm me.

Even if this was a trick, the fact that this "beast" was sentient, intelligent, and had any emotions to speak of meant that we had done him a terrible wrong in capturing him in this way. There were rules and laws, even about taking an enemy prisoner. Laws we were not following.

What happens when I remove the collar?

You will save me from a great deal of pain.

It was like a wall came down. He let a tiny trickle through of the agony he'd been experiencing since the collar was placed around his neck. That second heart inside me expanded, and I realized he had been protecting me from his pain.

I gasped and covered my mouth, hoping I hadn't made too much noise. With little further consideration, I reached my arms into the cage and toward his neck. His skin was more leathery than I'd expected, not the rough texture of the volcanic rock it resembled.

The collar itself was constructed of magefrost and steel-crystal. Its metal clasp was sealed inside the magefrost, accessible only with magic.

I withdrew my hands and gripped them together, took a deep breath, and closed my eyes. With Morros nearing full-ness overhead, I had access to more power than at other times of the lunar cycle. The seaglass gems braided into my hair and the small one on a pendant around my neck allowed me to channel Morros's power. Theoretically. I focused intently, directing my will toward the collar and pushing. My gems began to hum softly with power.

It was working! In moments, the magefrost around the collar's clasp melted away, revealing the mechanism. I gave it a push with a tiny chunk of ice and it released, causing the entire collar to fall onto the sand.

Pride filled my chest, inflating me like a pufferfish. I opened my eyes, and my gaze caught on the beast. Between us, the air shuddered like the intake of breath, and then his enormous body began to ripple. The dark lava of his thick skin softened, taking on a molten form. The thick horns curving away from his head split and undulated. His entire body glowed red-orange and a cascade of steam rose between us, blocking him from view.

Within a few seconds, the steam cleared. My jaw hung open. Before me was a man, no longer a beast. A large man, to be sure, with deep, mahogany brown skin and thick fiery-colored locs hanging past his shoulders. The subtle echo of fiery wings flashed behind him in their retracted state. He was pure beauty, with full lips framed by a neat dark mustache and goatee, a regal nose, and dark brown eyes. Those eyes had just a hint of fire behind them and were watching me carefully.

9

keeran

HER EYES ARE SO WIDE and round they resemble moons. But instead of fear wafting from her like acrid mist, I sense wonder. Excitement, even. Something deep within my chest loosens. She has not rejected me yet.

Now that the intense pain of the collar is gone, I take several deep breaths. The enchantment mimicked the power that had trapped me in that form. It is nice to be in my own skin again.

Questions dance in her eyes and I know I need to answer them, but I take another moment to breathe with my own lungs and feel the night air on my natural skin.

I sense the guard behind me. His even breathing lets me know he's fallen asleep standing up. Niara and I have time to talk for a bit.

She casts her gaze around and begins to gather herself,

straightening her shoulders. *What . . . what are you?* she asks in my mind.

My name is Keeran. I am the youngest son of the Ember Fae King. The form I took before is a result of the Obsidian Curse.

You're an Ember Fae prince? Her mental voice is shocked. Dismayed.

Which part of that bothers you more? My mouth pulls into a smile—an unfamiliar feeling.

All of it. She waves her hand vaguely. *Why were you cursed?*

I lean forward, breathing in her scent. My cursed form has a relatively poor sense of smell, but Ember Fae senses are extremely heightened. Niara smells of ginger and cinnamon, with hints of the salt of the sea. The scent calls to me in a way nothing else has, and I let it wash over me before I begin my tale.

Generations ago, an Ember Fae king desired to be blessed by the fire moon Ignis. My ancestor vowed devotion, promising that his youngest child would always serve as the Moon Child, channeling Ignis's magic into obsidian and using these powerful talismans to ensure prosperity and good fortune for the kingdom. This lasted for many solars, and we were blessed. But my grandfather was greedy, and instead of accepting the gift of the blessing, asked his Moon Child son to steal the power of Ignis.

How would he do that? she asks.

Limits were placed onto how much of Ignis's power could be channeled. My grandfather sought to have his son, my uncle, funnel enough magic from the moon to fill the entire Obsidian Oculus. The entire chamber would have become a talisman giving its wielder near unlimited power.

Her lips round to form an "O."

Exactly. It was right after the Oculus Accords were signed, and my grandfather, though he signed the treaty, had no real wish to share the holy site with your people.

My uncle did as he was instructed and attempted to channel a massive amount of power into the Oculus. Of course, Ignis was not pleased at this faithlessness. In retaliation, our great moon cursed the bloodline. Each youngest child, when we come of age, must be sacrificed to the volcano and transformed into the creature you saw.

She presses both hands against her mouth, tears welling in her eyes. My arms twitch, wanting to reach out and comfort her, but I cannot. Not yet.

My father had seen what had befallen his beloved youngest brother and hoped he could spare me. He tried to bargain with Ignis to no avail. On my twentieth solar, I transformed into the beast.

The memory of that first painful transformation comes over me and I wince. I had rampaged through the castle grounds, not quite believing what was happening to me. It had taken a dozen kings guards to subdue me, and then my family tearfully transported me to the Oculus.

Deep within the volcano, I exist in a sort of hibernated state. I'm aware of the passage of time, but . . . Tears drip down her face. It's agonizing not to be able to wipe them away for her.

But what? she asks.

But I am not in pain.

She sniffles and scrubs her cheeks with her palm. *How long have you been in the volcano?*

Ten solars. During our rituals, I'm able to speak with my family and learn some of the events of the day. You do not need to cry for me.

She shakes her head, and her multitude of braids tinkle, the little glass beads on their ends like chimes. *What made you come out during the Day One ritual?* she asks.

The warmth within me at being near to her, at seeing all of her little reactions, cools. I look down at the ground, my hands tightening into fists. *I was summoned,* I tell her. *One of your people somehow got hold of an ancient ritual and brought me out of my sleep.*

Her body grows rigid. Astonishment is quickly followed by anger—an intense rage that I did not believe Water Mages could access. Their entire society is based on following the principles of Morros: introspection, adaptability, calm, and balance. The historical cause of conflict between our two peoples has been rooted in the Water Mages' lack of intensity. For Ember Fae, passion is the point of existence. Morros is meant to temper the heat of Ignis, but we, Ignis's children, were meant to burn.

Niara, I am in your debt for releasing me. You have my deepest thanks. I reach my hand forward until it barely grazes the edge of the water cage. She blinks rapidly, staring at it, before reaching her arm through the barrier and grasping my forearm.

Her skin is cool, mine is warm. Where we touch, a tiny, sizzling column of steam rises. She sucks in a breath. The draw I feel toward her is so intense it frightens me, scares me. I cannot tell her everything I know, but . . .

The sound of footsteps approaching causes the guard nearby to jolt to wakefulness. *You must go now. Someone is coming.*

Her gaze darts around, and she releases my hand. My fingers shiver at the loss of contact.

What will you do now? she asks.

As she stands, I concentrate on the heat within me and ripple, transforming back into the beast. Without the magic of the collar, I have control. I can stay in human form for short periods, but being away from the volcano is slowly draining me. I don't tell Niara this. I grasp the collar, which is now just an inert piece of jewelry, and replace it around my neck.

At her confused expression I smile, knowing the display of sharp teeth is frightening in this form but that she will not be afraid. *I will bide my time until I know who summoned me and why.*

She retreats, walking backward into the shadows. *Will you come back tomorrow night?* I ask her.

The darkness swallows her before she responds. Her simple *Yes* causes my heart to beat faster. I will be waiting.

10

niara

THE FIFTH DAY of the Holy Convergence dawned with twin halos around the mother and daughter suns, a rare and unexpected phenomenon that the Order would no doubt interpret as an auspicious sign. For me, it felt like a warning —bright rings of fire watching me from above.

I'd barely slept after returning from my encounter with Keeran. An Ember Fae prince. First cursed as a young man and then summoned by Water Mages against his will. That meant one of *us* wanted him captured. Someone knew exactly who and what he was. But who could it be?

Only a priest or priestess would have the ability to channel enough power in order to summon an Ember Fae. As much as I wanted to entrust High Priestess Valya with this information, part of me was afraid. Could it have been her? She *was* the most powerful Mage. And if she wasn't the culprit, as I desperately hoped, would she believe me?

I decided that I needed to speak with Amal again. As the High Warden, he was tasked with our protection and security. While he was a martial arts expert, his magecraft was not such that he could have summoned Keeran. The threat the traitor posed to the Mages was great, and he would certainly have better ideas on how to flush this person out.

As the camp was being struck, I moved purposefully through the flotilla. The vessels were anchored close together, connected by floating walkways that bobbed gently with the waves. When we departed, they would be retracted, but they aided in loading and offloading all the camp supplies.

The wardens usually kept to a predictable schedule, doing training and drills in the hour after breaking their fast. I spotted Safina going through the forms of Fluidhand, her lithe body making the martial art look like a dance. I gave her a wave and scanned the soldiers for the High Warden, but he was nowhere to be found.

Safina, probably sensing my distress and urgency, left her row to meet me on the floating bridge.

"Have you seen Amal?" I asked her.

"He and Priestess Ylena were heading toward the curator skiffs earlier. Why?"

"It's, umm . . ." I wanted to tell her everything, but I spotted the Second Warden glaring in our direction. I couldn't get my best friend into trouble right now. "We'll talk later. I've got something big to tell you, but I need to speak with Amal first."

She nodded, still concerned, and squeezed my shoulder before returning to the deck of the galleon.

The three curator skiffs normally surrounded the High

Curator's massive schooner and, as far as I knew, contained mainly offices and study rooms. It seemed an odd place for Ylena and Amal to have a meeting. Two of the vessels were in their normal location, while the last had been moored at the edge of the flotilla, away from the bustle of the main ships. Something about that felt odd to me, so I decided to check there first.

I approached slowly on the floating walkway, noticing the lack of activity. The other ships were being loaded with equipment, but this one was suspiciously quiet. So quiet that I could hear voices rising from an interior room. I circled to the port side, where a porthole's rusty latch had come a loose, cracking it open a sliver.

"If you can't get this done—" Amal was saying.

"If you weren't changing things every other day, we wouldn't have to—" That was Ylena, sounding irritated as usual.

"Do you need me to speak slower? Because I will." Amal's tone was mocking. "It's an ancient text. Written in verse. In an arcane language. The meanings of some passages are open for interpretation. The Second Curator said—"

"You brought the Second Curator into this?" Ylena hissed.

"I asked her an abstract question, framing it as a thought experiment. She said our original interpretation was too modern. The translation of 'Solareth vheren'kai trehal drahal' as 'Fire is captured before the ultimate end' more likely refers to the night before the final day instead of the final day. So we need to act on the second to last night of the Holy Convergence."

I pressed closer to the ship's hull, heart hammering against my ribs. What were they planning for the second to last day?

Ylena groaned. "Moving things up an entire day will be very difficult."

"None of this has been easy. Did you think it would be?"

"I still think the risks you take are too big. First breaking into the archives, now consulting one of the curators?"

"I told you, the Ember Fae archives were in disarray after the earthquake in Ashcrest. My presence wasn't registered since they employed Water Mages to plug the plumbing leaks and fix the flood damage."

I bit back a gasp. The ancient text the Ember Fae guards were searching for—it was Amal who had stolen it. Beneath my feet, the floorboards of the walkway groaned and whined.

"So here is what you will do, my dear priestess." Amal's voice grew low and coaxing. "Use that beautiful brain of yours to adjust your plans. And don't worry too much about the consequences. When we're done draining the cursed Fae prince of all the Fire Moon's power, we will overthrow Valya, install you as High Priestess, and fix everything wrong with the Order. With strong leadership and vision—leadership that remembers what the Ember Fae did to our ancestors instead of being willing to placate them—we'll start the work of restoring our people to their rightful place as rulers of Emberglade. I know that you can do what needs to be done, my dear. And everything will work out just as we planned."

My hands trembled. Treason. They were planning a

coup against Valya—using "the cursed Fae prince," Keeran, as a weapon.

The two went quiet, and I strained to hear. Then my stomach curdled in disgust when I made out the wet sounds of kissing.

Ylena's voice spoke first. "You need to remember you belong to me, Amal. I don't like seeing you toying with that little failure of an acolyte. We don't need her for anything."

I sucked in a breath, my blood turning to ice.

Amal chuckled, the sound totally devoid of warmth. "Niara? Valya trusts her implicitly. I still think it's best to keep her close . . . For the time being."

"So it's strategy, then?" Ylena sounded amused. "Not just a taste for damaged goods?"

"She is pretty and naïve," Amal replied dismissively, stabbing a shard of ice into my chest. "And considering she has some kind of strange connection to our fire beast, she may be even more useful that I previously thought. But the hour grows late, my dear. We can't afford to tarry. I'll leave first, so we're not spotted together again."

I scrambled to back away from the window, stumbling on a loose board on the walkway. I was just steadying myself and beating a hasty retreat when a voice called my name.

"Niara?"

I turned to find Amal's handsome face arranged in a look of pleasant surprise that didn't reach his eyes. Taking a deep breath, I summoned every bit of control I possessed, forced my lips into a coy smile, and looked up at him through my lashes.

"High Warden." I crafted my voice to sound breathless.

"I was hoping to find you alone. After our conversation yesterday . . . well, I couldn't stop thinking about what you said about . . . deepening our acquaintance."

Pretty and naïve. He didn't think much of me, so I tried my best to give him what he expected. Stepping closer, I put a little extra sway in my hips. "Perhaps we could arrange a time for later to . . . get closer?"

Amal studied my face carefully. I held my breath, wondering if my racing heart would give me away. Then his stern expression smoothed into a charming smile. "Yes, that would be most agreeable. This evening, let's plan to meet after last meal."

"I'll be looking forward to it all day," I whispered as seductively as I could manage, and then turned to walk away.

I moved at a measured pace, feeling his eyes on my back. Only when I was on the shore once more, hidden behind a stack of crates, did I allow my knees to give way. I crumpled onto the sand, body shaking with pain and fury as the reality of their betrayal washed over me.

Amal and Ylena had stolen the Ember Fae text. They had summoned Keeran. They were planning to overthrow Valya. And all this time, Amal had been manipulating me, using my feelings, laughing at me behind my back.

Niara? Keeran's voice touched my mind, gentle with concern. *Your distress—I can feel it. What's wrong?*

I pressed my palms against my eyes, trying to steady my breathing. *I know who summoned you,* I replied. *The High Warden and one of the priestesses. They're planning to use you in some sort of ritual in two nights to steal your power and overthrow our High Priestess.*

There was a pause, and hot anger sparked in that second heart within me that belonged to him. *How did you learn this?*

I overheard them. I'm not sure if they suspect that I know.

Then you might be in danger, he responded.

They underestimate me. My thoughts raced. If I told Valya, would she believe me over the High Warden? If I confided in Safina, would I be putting her in danger? I wasn't sure who to trust with this, but one thing was certain—I needed to get Keeran away from here as soon as possible.

Be ready tonight, I told him, rising to my feet and straightening my shoulders. For the first time in my life, the turbulent emotions within me—the anger, the betrayal, the outrage—didn't feel like weaknesses to be suppressed. They felt like fuel for a fire that had been waiting to ignite.

11

niara

THAT NIGHT there were no dreams because I did not sleep. I lay on my pallet staring up at the sliver of sky I could see through the smoke hole in our tent. A smattering of stars interrupted the blackness of the night. I replayed the conversation I'd overheard between Amal and Ylena over and over again, trying to wrap my head around the fact that they could be involved in this kind of conspiracy.

Due to the drain of maintaining Keeran's cage, Valya had gone into sequestration a whole day early. Normally a half day's meditation was required by the High Priestess before the Day Six ceremony, since it was the most involved and intense one. I'd desperately wanted to speak to her, to warn her of what I'd learned, and face whatever consequences may come, but she'd been deep in meditation, a state that left her essentially comatose and unable to be awoken early.

It had meant my duties for the day were limited, but of course I'd used the extra time to worry. If Amal and Ylena got their way, there would certainly be war. Not only would people I cared about die, but many, many more all across our land. I needed to do all I could in order to stop it.

The women I shared the tent with were all breathing deeply, in the embrace of sleep. When no one had stirred for two hours, I rose on wobbling legs and left the tent. Resolve plus the fiery, bubbling anger within me fueled every step I took.

I crossed the camp cautiously, avoiding every warden I saw, until I reached Keeran's prison. As usual, he was positioned at the edge of the sandy shoreline, where it met the waist-high grasses. He looked up at my approach, eyes glowing orange-red. His beastly face was solemn.

I had borrowed one of Valya's largest seaglass gems for tonight. Usage by someone other than a priestess was forbidden, but with her out of commission, I hadn't been able to ask for permission. I would need it to channel as much of Morros's power as possible.

The Melancholic Guardian was several nights away from being completely full, and overhead, the cloudless sky revealed him in all of his glory. However, that meant the camp was relatively brightly lit for the middle of the night. Thankfully, there were no guards stationed directly near Keeran's prison at the moment.

I crouched on the sand in front of him and pulled the gem from my pocket. It was smaller than the egg-sized one Valya wore around her neck, but larger than the marble-sized ones the other priestesses bore. Nestled in the palm of my hand, it glowed a soft blue-green in the moonlight.

A gust of wind kicked up, causing the tall grasses nearby to bend and sway. I took a deep breath and regarded the cursed prince. *I'm going to release you tonight. You'll need to get as far away from here as possible*, I told him mentally.

What about you? his deep voice rumbled through my head.

Don't worry about me. If they get their hands on you and do this ancient spell they found, they'll drain you of your power. If it's anything like The Tragedy of Goldensky and Flickerfeet, *that would kill you, wouldn't it?*

His eyes sparked. *You've read our fairy tales? Yes, I believe they must have been talking about the Lunar Fire spell. Ignis is well known for his curses. By using Lunar Fire, anyone could drain the Fire Moon's power from one He has cursed. It was locked in the archive because it is forbidden. And if they succeed, I would not survive.*

My heart thundered in my chest.

But I cannot leave you behind, he said. *They will certainly know it was you who freed me.*

Frustration bubbled within me. *It doesn't matter if they know. What matters is their plot doesn't succeed and you get away.*

It matters to me, Niara. You matter *to me.*

Not only could I sense the sincerity in his mental voice, but I could feel it pulsing within me through our emotional bond. *Why?* I asked. *Why do we have this connection?*

His fiery gaze darted away. *I will tell you once I am free. If you come along with me.*

I snorted. *Where would we go? My entire life is the Order. It has been since I was a child.*

You will not be safe here once they unmask you. His voice was implacable.

When High Priestess Valya emerges from her meditation, she will protect me. I hoped.

But I was a failed Water Mage acolyte with no family and nowhere to go. Freeing Keeran would stop the overthrow of the Order that I loved and the war that would surely follow. But where would it leave me? Dead? In prison? I hadn't thought that far ahead. The chance that I would be heralded as a hero seemed low, but allowing Amal and Ylena to continue with their plan was impossible.

I shook my head, knowing that I wasn't going to convince Keeran of anything. I needed to move forward with freeing him before it was too late. Focusing on the large gem in my hands, I worked to channel Morros's power. Overcoming High Priestess Valya's enchantment on the water cage would be difficult, but now was the perfect time, since in her current meditative state, she would not be able to reinforce the magecraft. I just needed a crack to exploit.

I sank into the power, doing my best to funnel everything I could into the gem. The smooth seaglass cooled in my palm, letting me know it was working. It connected with my other seaglass gems, the ones in my hair and around my neck. With them, I sensed the cage, the boundaries of it, and found a weakness, a tiny area where it was thinner than other places, where Valya's exhaustion was starting to show through.

I pushed at the weak spot, deteriorating it further until it became a minuscule hole within the water cage too tiny to see. Little by little, I made the hole larger, retracting the stronger barrier around it. I felt Keeran sense the opening.

Experimentally, he stuck a clawed finger through and touched the sand on the other side. All I had to do was make the breach wider, enough for him to get through.

Sweat broke out on my brow. I was reaching the limits of my water magic abilities, but I had to push forward. I could not fail. The stakes were too high. The tiny fissure in the cage grew larger and larger until it was the size of Beast Keeran's head. He peered at me through the gap and then froze.

Niara, get out of here now. They're coming.

But I couldn't stop.

Niara. Keeran's voice in my head was insistent.

I have to get you free first. See if you can wiggle through.

You must leave now! he boomed at me, but I held fast. The opening was nearly large enough for his wide shoulders. That was all he needed.

The sound of feet racing across the sand broke my concentration. Rough hands wrenched my right arm, causing me to drop the gem. My left arm was gripped with a gentler touch. I looked over to find Safina, tears welling in her eyes.

Wardens surrounded the cage. The tall man on my right side glared down at me with menace. Amal stepped through the line of guards to face me.

"I'm not entirely sure what you are trying to do here, First Tidemaiden," he said, his voice sounding honestly confused. "But freeing this creature that tried to kill us all is treason."

"He's not a creature! He's a man!" I yelled. I turned to Safina. "His name is Keeran, he's a cursed Ember Fae p—"

But my words were cut off when a water mask was affixed to my face.

"I cannot allow you to infect anyone else with your treasonous speech," Amal said. "It's a shame that the rigors and stresses of the Order's initiation process have brought you to this, Niara. We all held out great hope that you would become an adequate priestess one day. I know Valya certainly did. She will be most disappointed in you."

He bent to pick up the gem that had fallen when the wardens grabbed me. "We shall have to add theft to the list of your crimes, along, of course, with treason against the Order of Morros."

Amal turned, his face limned with moonlight that made it glow. Behind him in the cage, Keeran appeared to grow larger and fill the space more completely.

"Due to the Holy Convergence and the need for all the Archons to be in Solmane for the tournament and the royal wedding next week, we will not have time for a traditional tribunal. In cases of unequivocal treason, it is my prerogative as High Warden to sentence you to the Unmooring."

Beside me, Safina gasped.

"In the morning, you will be bound on an unsteerable craft with one day's worth of provisions and left to the fate of the sea. May Morros have mercy on you." He sounded like he truly regretted having to pass this sentence, the fiend. A single tear dripped down Safina's face.

"Take her away," Amal ordered, and the male warden on my right jostled me, marching me away from Keeran. Safina had to keep up. My last glimpse of Keeran was of the dark lava of his skin glowing orange all over.

His roar split open the night. It was so anguished and

furious that it caused my very bones to vibrate. The male guard, who was squeezing my arm too tightly, stumbled on the sand.

I had failed, again, and now it wasn't just me who would pay the price.

12

keeran

NIARA!

I scream her name in my mind as they drag her away from me. My claws rake uselessly against the water barrier, each desperate swipe sending ripples across its surface but doing nothing to break it. Through our connection, her fear and desperation slice against me like a knife.

I'm so sorry, she repeats over and over again. Then she's gone from my view, obscured by the large tents of the camp. The High Warden follows, his arrogant stride and self-satis-fied smile burning into my memory. I will tear him apart for this. I will reduce him to ash.

But first, I need to get to her.

I batter at the cage for the rest of the night, calling out to Niara mentally, but she doesn't respond. Her emotions are a whirlwind of fear, shame, and anger. I whisper words of comfort to her, hoping they penetrate, but not sure they are. It's like she has already given up.

As dawn breaks, the camp bustles with activity. The flotilla prepares to depart, and I remain trapped in this watery prison. Wardens cast wary glances my way as they load the final supplies onto the ships. None approach too closely. They fear me—as they should.

Just like every other day since my capture, a group of Order priests and priestesses levitates my cage and places it below the decks of one of their sea crafts. I'm shut in the dark during the day with only the sound of the sea and the presence of small rodents for company.

The ship vibrates as the anchor rises, and then we are moving. Niara's emotions burst in a new flurry of fear. I probe our connection, feeling it stretched taut like a thread of heated glass. The pressure builds at the back of my skull, a dull throb that promises worse to come.

It is undeniable proof of what I've sensed since I was first forced out of the volcano. We are fated mates. It is the rarest of bonds among my people, and somehow, I've started the twining with a Water Mage.

As the flotilla continues its journey west, the discomfort I've been feeling all morning blooms into pain, sharp and insistent. Each foot of distance between me and my mate is a new torture. We cannot be separated. Especially not now, so soon after the twining bond has begun to form.

My breathing grows ragged. Sweat beads on my skin, evaporating instantly against the heat of my body. I close my eyes and see flashes—imagining what Niara is going through based on her emotions: her small body lying on a small raft. The meager single day of food and water essentially a death sentence as she drifts along the Aurelian Sea.

She will not understand the pain wracking her muscles and bones. She won't know why her body is betraying her this way.

The distance between us grows. The pain intensifies.

Something within me cracks open, a fault line of rage and desperation. The magic of the curse that has been my burden for ten solars surges and shifts, reacting with the magic of the twining. Ember Fae mates have been known to perform incredible feats in order to save their other halves. I wrangle hold of this collision of powers, gripping it with everything I have inside of me.

Those who have separated me from my mate must pay.

In response to my emotion and will, my cursed form shifts and grows larger than the beast ever has before. The water cage, designed to contain a creature of a certain size, begins to strain.

Fire erupts from deep within me as I tap into a wellspring of primal magic that I've never felt before. The flames shoot outward in all directions, evaporating the spelled water that has been holding me captive. The cage is gone, and I sit on the wooden floorboards of the ship.

Steam fills the air, scalding and thick. I claw at the wood. It chars and splinters under my touch as the beast grows larger still. Then I stand, fists raised above me, and punch. The wooden ceiling shatters. I leap onto the deck of the ship above.

Wardens shout in alarm, hastily conjuring magefrost weapons that glitter like stars in the morning light. They throw spears and arrows at me, but the tips and blades melt before they make contact, droplets of water sizzling against my thick hide.

I throw my head back and release a roar that carries all my fury and pain. The sound is deafening, inhuman. The sea around the ship begins to bubble and boil, more steam rising to create a thick, impenetrable fog. The wardens' voices grow panicked as visibility drops to nothing.

I flex my muscles and flames shoot out of my skin, searing the very flammable ship. The vessel groans and shudders beneath me. The water churns violently as parts of the ship begin to break away and sink.

Chaos erupts. As fire races across the deck, some of the crew leap into the boiling water. Their magecraft will probably save them from the scalding waves. Meanwhile, the wardens stand their ground and fight, hurling weapons that do little more than annoy me in this state. I am beyond pain now. I am rage incarnate, a force of destruction born of desperation and need.

"Keeran!"

A voice cuts through the roaring in my ears. Female, authoritative, but not Niara. I whirl around, ready to incinerate anyone who dares approach me.

Through the billowing steam, a figure emerges. It's the female warden who stood at Niara's side, the one whose tears betrayed her true feelings. She stands on a section of deck that hasn't yet caught fire, her hands raised in a gesture of peace rather than preparing to attack.

"Keeran, stop! You want to save Niara, right?"

Her words are like cold water on my rage. Niara. Yes. This destruction serves no purpose if it doesn't bring me closer to her.

"I can help you reach her," the woman continues, her voice steady despite the fear I can smell coming off her in waves. "But you need to control yourself."

I struggle against the beast, against the curse, against the pain of separation that threatens to drive me mad. A particularly sharp pulse through our bond nearly brings me to my knees—Niara is suffering, and I'm wasting time with this senseless destruction. The High Warden is nowhere in sight. Were he here, then perhaps enacting my vengeance would make sense.

With monumental effort, I begin to shift, forcing my body back toward human form. But this far from the Obsidian Oculus, taking my natural shape is like swimming against a current of molten metal, every inch of progress agony. However, I push through, focusing on Niara's face in my mind.

Finally, I stand before this Water Mage as a man, not a monster, though flames still lick at my skin and my eyes burn with inner fire. The ship continues to burn around us, tilting dangerously as water floods its lower decks.

"What is your name?" I ask her.

"Safina. Niara is my best friend."

I nod. "Thank you, Safina."

"There's a small boat on the far side," Safina says, already moving. "Follow me."

I stagger after her, weakness hitting me now that the rage has subsided. The pain of separation remains, a constant throb in my bones. We reach a small craft, barely big enough for one person, tied to the sinking ship.

"Get in," she commands. "And take this." She tosses me a rough cloth sack. "Figure out how to . . . cover up."

The transformation leaves me naked, and I wrap the sack around my waist.

"I'll enchant the dinghy with a tracking spell. It will take you directly to her."

"You're not coming?" I ask, my voice rough from the roaring. "She will surely ask after you."

She firms her lips. "I need to stay. I can delay anyone who might follow you." She grasps hold of a bracelet of blue and green beads around her wrist and takes a deep breath, her eyes growing unfocused with concentration. Beneath her hand, the bracelet begins to glow.

"Go now," she says.

"Why are you helping me?" I manage to ask as I climb into the craft.

Safina's eyes meet mine, determination shining in them. "Niara is my sister in all but blood. She risked everything to save you, and I would do anything for her. Now go. The spell won't last forever."

She cuts the rope tethering the little boat, which immediately begins to move, cutting through the water at an unnatural speed, away from the burning wreckage and toward shore. Toward Niara.

I collapse at the bottom of the craft, fighting to maintain human form as the distance between us begins to close.

Hold on, Niara. I'm coming.

13

niara

I AWOKE to a tickle of smoke against my nose. One by one, my other senses came back online. I lay on the sand, but my head rested on something more solid. I could sense light against my eyelids, and I blinked them open to find the magenta glow of dawn cresting the horizon.

Next to me were the dying embers of a fire that still produced enough warmth to cut through the early morning chill. And above me, Keeran's face peered down. Dark eyes crinkled in a soft smile.

The events of the day before rushed back to me. I'd been floating aimlessly on the small raft given to those sentenced to the Unmooring. The sun's rays beat down on me, searing my skin. Pain wracked my body in waves. I knew I would need to ration my one day of supplies and had been taking only small sips of water from the canteen, but my shaking hands had spilled it on the boards of the raft.

Melancholy had been an anchor around my neck, making me perhaps closer to Morros than I ever had been, when I spotted something cutting through the waves swiftly toward me.

Fear trapped a scream in my throat, but I quickly recognized the tiny boat as one of ours. Then I spotted him. Keeran. His expression was one of fierce determination as he raced my way.

My scream turned into a squeal of relief. The pain faded immediately, and I embraced him when he reached me. He lifted me into his arms and sat me on his lap—the only way we could both fit in the small craft. He told me of Safina's aid and how she had stayed behind. I worried over the consequences she would face.

As her spell had run out once he located me, Keeran had to row us to shore, which was still visible in the distance, thank Morros. We ended up here on the beach, where I collapsed. Both of us were exhausted. We split the rest of my rations, and I fell immediately into a deep, dreamless sleep.

Now, fully awake, I sat up to face Keeran. He yawned, stretching. He wore only a scrap of fabric tied around his waist—the remnants of some kind of bag. My cheeks heated. I wasn't sure where to look; there was just so much of him.

His densely muscled chest, smooth and nearly hairless, was lightly covered with sand. Powerful thighs and thick calves begged to be admired. His wings were just a ghostly apparition of fire behind him, nearly invisible in the light.

He reached out and stroked my face gently, his expression more than just one of fondness. There was admiration there as well.

"You came for me," I whispered.

"Of course." He dropped his hand and averted his gaze. "There's something I must tell you." At his pause and body language, my nerves grew. "I had been fairly certain before, but when we were separated, it became undeniable."

"What did?" I asked.

His eyes found mine. They were so dark, I felt lost in their depths.

"You and I are fated mates, Niara. We have begun the twining."

I blinked, searching his face for any sign he was jesting.

"That is why it hurt so badly to be separated," he continued. "Especially at this early stage. Even a mile is too much. It will get better within a few months, and especially after we complete the ceremony—that is, *if* we complete the ceremony," he said, looking away again.

I was frozen, unsure how to respond. Of all of the stories I'd read about Ember Fae mates, none of them had included a partner who was not Fae.

"How can we be fated when I'm a Water Mage?" I finally asked, pushing the words out of a throat grown impossibly dry.

"The only theory I have is that you must have Ember Fae ancestry somewhere. You've been struggling with your water magic? I've heard it spoken of around the camp. Perhaps the water and the fire in your background have been in conflict."

I was all too aware of how easily every other initiate to the Order took to magecraft and how difficult it had always been for me to conjure anything simple. Each failure of my trials had been a cause of such misery and shame. If there *were* an Ember Fae in my family lineage, it would all make so much more sense.

Due to the conflict between our peoples, there had not been unions very often, but it must have happened occasionally. I'd never known my grandparents, and my parents had been gone for well over fifteen solars—there was no one to ask, and our family had not been auspicious enough to be tracked in the curators' records.

Suddenly, Keeran shuddered. His eyes flashed brightly with the molten fire of the beast. He gritted his teeth and clenched his fists, the veins in his neck standing out in bold relief.

"What's wrong?" I asked, leaning forward to grasp his arm.

"This far from the Oculus, it's difficult to hold this form," he said through ragged breaths.

"Well then transform back," I cried.

"I fear the beast will lose control."

I frowned. "You never have before."

The pain seemed to fade, and the corner of his lips quirked up. "You didn't see me when the flotilla set sail, separating the two of us. I destroyed one of their ships."

My brows rose. "I wish I could have witnessed that. Any chance you took down High Warden Amal?"

The brief amusement on his face died. "No. But I will. I vow it." He took my hands in his and squeezed gently. "Without the water cage, traveling in the cursed form would be difficult. It was created to live inside the volcano. I could very well set fire to the landscape, making us even easier to track."

"Do you think they're tracking us?" I asked.

"If they planned to carry out a coup using me to channel Ignis's magic, then they cannot afford to let me go. Also, allowing a rampaging fire beast loose in the countryside is poor form."

He looked around, scenting the air. "I think we must be in Thyraelis. We've certainly traveled west for long enough."

"Can you seek sanctuary or aid from the Fae here?"

His expression grew cautious. "Though the Fireforged are distant relatives, they will be suspicious of anyone cursed by Ignis. And the Rootborn Earth Fae are our natural enemies. I think it best to avoid both of them."

"I'm not sure what we do now," I told him, melancholy seeping into my bones. "Should we try to get back to your family in Ashcrest?" That seemed the best option, though I didn't know how it could be accomplished. We'd have to travel across two separate nations, and if Amal and the rest of the Water Mages were searching for us, our chances of success were low.

Keeran shook his head slowly. "I believe our best option is to break the curse."

I leaned back, pulling my hands from his, surprise stealing my voice.

"According to my father," he continued, "at the same time that Ignis cursed our line, the palace seer received the following prophecy: *Where Ignis's power meets Lyra's light, and tempers yield to wisdom's might, devotion true, the curse must prove, with twining vows to his only love.*"

My heartbeat sped up. "So you need your fated mate to break the curse."

He held my gaze. "Ignis's power meets Lyra's light only at a very specific celestial event."

Understanding dawned. "Day Seven of the Holy Convergence!"

Keeran's expression was grim.

"The eclipse is visible at certain Fire Moon temples. In Thyraelis, the only temples used for that purpose are near the towns of Neufall, Belward, and Flamescar."

"Day Seven is when Amal and Ylena intended to drain you," I said.

"Yes. The only good thing to come out of their treachery was that it gives me the opportunity that my uncle never had . . . to find my mate and break this curse."

My stomach began to quiver. "This . . . this seems like a lot of responsibility." Keeran was a prince. He was likely used to responsibility, but I had only ever been a disappointment.

Feeling my distress, he took my hands again. "We do not have to complete the twining ceremony, Niara. I am not trying to trap you in a mating you do not want. The prophecy states only that *I* must make the vows, not that you must reciprocate. If you do not want this, once the curse is broken, I can sever our bond. I would never force you into a lifelong commitment you have no wish to join."

He'd misunderstood the nature of my emotions, but I wasn't quite ready to correct him yet. "What happens to you if the twining is severed?"

Keeran blinked rapidly and averted his eyes once more. "That does not matter. All that matters is that you have a choice."

His answer was not satisfying, and his evasion let me know that the consequences for him would not be pleasant. The fairy tales never mentioned severing a bond. However, I was still wrapping my mind around what it meant that we were fated.

"Fine. Let's focus on breaking the curse first. Do you know how close we are to one of these three temples?"

"No. But it should be easy enough to find out."

"While also avoiding most of the locals?" I raised a brow.

"It would definitely be best to avoid the Fireforged."

"Are the Rootborn Fae any friendlier?"

He took a deep breath. "Friendly is rather a strong term. Slightly less overtly murderous might be a better way to put it."

Oh joy.

14

niara

KEERAN AND I HEADED INLAND, searching for a road. Within a few hours, we found a well-used path but kept to the tree line on the lookout for any Fireforged Fae.

Maintaining his human form was growing more and more difficult for him. His breathing grew labored and sweat peppered his forehead. I forced us to take regular rest breaks. Fortunately, my meager magecraft was enough to find nearby water and fill our canteen from a few feet away.

At one point, we came across a campsite in a forest clearing that looked to have been abandoned in a hurry. In their rush, they'd left behind a sack of well-used clothing. I dug through to find a pair of pants and a cloak that fit Keeran's large proportions, though all the shirts were far too small. Still, the brown cloak's hood covered his bright hair and allowed us to blend in better with the flora.

Throughout the morning, a few lone travelers passed in

motorized contraptions or on dark-furred gredanes trotting along happily. One brave soul even rode a shaggy, single-horned shukan. I made sure to keep a wide berth of that particular creature.

Though we followed the road, which must eventually lead to a town, we had no idea if we were headed toward or away from one of Ignis's temples, or if we were near one at all. We were in a foreign land, with no coin, no allies, and Keeran was growing weaker all the time.

My spirits were sinking low when a large caravan of travelers approached. Their brightly colored autowagons adorned with bells and chimes marked them as Roamers—nomadic human entertainers who toured the lands giving impressive theatrical performances.

Though the Roamers had never been known to be in conflict with any of the many races on Lunaterra, they were a notoriously tight-knit group. I guessed that no Fireforged would be among their number, as Fae and humans rarely mixed.

Keeran was resting against a tree, his entire body covered in sweat. I made a split-second decision and raced up the embankment and onto the road while the first autowagon was still a hundred feet away.

"Niara, what are you doing?" his voice called out behind me, but it was already done.

The driver was a burly man in his middle years, with tawny skin and salt and pepper hair. I waved my arms over my head, and he obligingly slowed his vehicle.

"May the flow be upon you," I said automatically, then mentally kicked myself.

His brows climbed into his hairline. "Greetings, Water Mage. What brings you so far from home?"

"A sad circumstance. I was wondering if you might be able to tell me where this road leads. Is there a village nearby?" Hope laced my voice, but the deep exhaustion was also present.

"The town of Leafhollow is but eight miles yonder," he replied.

I held my breath. "And might that be close to either Neufall, Belward, or Flamescar?"

His smile was kind. "It is but half a day's ride from there to Belward."

Relief made my shoulders sag. "Thank you, kind sir. I am greatly appreciative."

"Would you like a ride, lass?" he asked.

"I have a companion, and he is ill." I motioned toward the trees. "Would you have room for two?"

Caution crossed his expression, but just then Keeran limped from the tree line. He very deliberately pulled down his hood to reveal his fiery orange-red hair.

This time the Roamer's surprise was somewhat muted, but from within the wagon, I heard a gasp. We had witnesses, though I'd expected as much.

"A Water Mage and Fireforged traveling together? This day certainly does hold surprises," the man said, and then invited us onto his wagon.

THE ROAMERS WERE A JOVIAL LOT, sharing jokes as well as food and water liberally. By the time they dropped us off at a large inn in busy Leafhollow, Keeran looked quite a bit better and my mood had lifted.

We thanked them profusely, and the driver, who'd introduced himself as Blossom, clasped my hands in his. "The Roamer ethos is to pay forward any kindness you receive twofold. That is all I ask in return."

I bowed my head. "I shall. May the Eternal Flow guide your journey."

"And yours as well, traveler."

And then they were gone in a cascade of competing bells.

The interior of the inn looked like the inside of a tree and must have been shaped by Rootborn Fae magic. The walls were living bark in hues of amber, chestnut, and mahogany with roots twining their way up walls. The ceiling overhead was a canopy of living leaves. The furniture appeared to have been grown and not built, with tables and benches emerging seamlessly from the floor.

I balked in the doorway, unsure whether this was a Rootborn establishment or not, but Keeran brushed past me, leaving me not much choice but to follow. As we had no coin, I was considering the best way to offer my services: washing dishes or cleaning rooms in exchange for a night's lodging. However, Keeran, careful to keep his hood up, approached the innkeeper, a grim-faced dark-skinned human man with shockingly amber eyes.

Keeran inclined his head, then spoke to the man in a language I'd never heard before. As the words tumbled from his mouth, the innkeeper's eyes widened and his face split into a toothy grin. He grew animated, and the two went back and forth, speaking like old friends.

Eventually, the man came from around the counter and led us up several sets of winding staircases made of roots to a room on the top level of the inn, one of the premium suites.

"What in Morros's name did you say to him? And what was that language?" I asked once we were alone in the suite's well-appointed sitting room.

"Atlanti. It's a language belonging to a small ethnic group who manages to survive in the Desert Deadlands. My dancing instructor was one of their people, so I learned their mother tongue. It's one of the most unforgiving languages on Lunaterra, and for an outsider to learn it essentially enters you into a small fraternity."

"It's very lucky that we came to this inn," I said.

"Not luck. While you were playing that hand-clapping game with the children, I asked Blossom about the various inns here and who ran them. From his description, I guessed the proprietor was Atlanti. He warned me off this one at first, but I asked to be dropped off here."

I sat back, impressed.

"And while the building was grown by the Rootborn, most of the inn's clientele are human. Which was another point in its favor."

I tilted my head. "The Roamers assumed that you were Fireforged. Aren't the Rootborn and Fireforged enemies? Wouldn't it be easier for you to blend in at a Fireforged establishment?"

"There's a high chance they could sense the curse on me. They worship Ignis, and any hint of Ignis's disfavor would put a target on my back. They would consider themselves honor-bound to eliminate me as a scourge."

I reared back. "How are you doing, anyway? How long will you be able to keep this form?"

The tension in his jaw grew more pronounced. "There's a small pond out back. Tonight, I will go there and transform. That will help."

"But doesn't the water hurt you?"

He winced. "Yes, but not as badly as staying human. And I will not risk damaging any property if I'm in the pond."

I didn't like the idea of him being in pain at all, but it wasn't like he was exactly comfortable right now.

Night fell, and the innkeeper brought us a large meal of savory vegetables, delicious soups, and warm, crusty bread. After we ate, Keeran slipped out and headed down to the pool.

I moved to the window overlooking the back of the inn to watch. Morros was nearly full, and three of his brother moons were also in their later stages, so the evening was bright.

Keeran disrobed quickly, giving me a very clear image of his powerful body in all its glory before he slipped into the water. Soon, steam rose from the pond's surface.

My forehead thunked against the thick glass as I leaned forward. I stepped back, rubbing the tender spot, glad no one was here to see me.

15

niara

KEERAN STAYED underwater for about a quarter of an hour before emerging in his human form again. When he came back into the suite, I was on the settee, pretending to read one of the books I found on the small shelf in the corner.

He sat next to me, and if he suspected that I had been watching from the window, he never said a word. We talked then, sharing our histories. I told him of growing up in the orphanage, of yearning to become a water priestess because of all the wonderful things the Order did for me after my parents died.

And then I did something I never had before. I told him about my parents, about life before the orphanage, when I was loved and cared for, when my home was full of joy and light and laughter and music. It hurt so much to think of those days. Some of the other children in the orphanage liked to speak of their families, but most of us didn't. I hadn't even shared these stories with Safina. But if Keeran was indeed my fated mate, and if we were actually going to complete the bond, then I wanted him to truly know every part of me.

For his part, he told me of growing up in the Ember King's castle in the capital of Ashcrest, of the day he understood what his fate would be as the youngest son. Of coming of age, having his moon day ceremony, and then being sacrificed to the flames. Of transforming that first time into the beast. How it felt to have his body shift and grow. To enter the lava and become one with it.

For years, he had been in a somewhat dormant state, cognizant of the passage of time but not of much else aside from ceremony days when his family would visit the Obsidian Oculus and he would emerge. Until the day he was summoned by traitorous Water Mages.

When I yawned loudly, then hurriedly covered my mouth, he chuckled. "We'd better get some rest."

The double doors were open to the sleeping chamber, where a large and cozy bed lay, especially inviting after days of sleeping on the hard ground on pallets.

In the washroom, preparing to scrub off the day's grime, I regarded myself in the mirror, searching for signs of any Ember Fae. My hair was darkest brown, and there had never been so much as a hint of wings flickering behind me. But I knew Keeran wasn't lying. The fact that I could speak to his beast in my mind, that even in his human form, his emotions were laid bare to me, and that being separated had caused me an agony I hadn't been familiar with before—we were fated. And even though he had offered a way to sever this growing bond, was that what I truly wanted?

The water running from the tap into the wash basin was cool. Being on the top floor, it would likely take quite a while for heated water from the inn's boiler to reach us. I concentrated on the basin. The seaglass gems in my hair and around my neck connected to Morros's power. I could *feel* the water.

I told it to heat.

Having no idea what I was doing, merely acting on some instinct that I half thought I'd invented, I raised my hands over the water, like some storybook witch over a cauldron. I pushed my intention and my will into the water.

Steam rose from its surface.

I stumbled back. Then moved forward again to dip my hands in. It was the temperature I preferred for bathing. The smile overtaking my face could not be contained. I washed, then changed into the nightgown that the innkeeper's staff had brought, along with changes of clothes for both of us and toiletries. Then I sped out into the bedroom.

Keeran had acquired a cot from somewhere and was spreading a blanket across it. "Niara, I wanted to tell—" But I cut off whatever he was going to say when I smashed into him, chest first, wrapped my arms around his neck, and kissed him.

His shock sizzled across our bond, the emotions much stronger now than ever before. But he got over the surprise quickly and wrapped his arms around me, pulling me even tighter to him as if trying to fuse our bodies together.

That's exactly what I wanted. This draw that had been growing over the past few days was jarring in its intensity.

Instead of trying to fight it or even spending one more moment second-guessing the whys of it, I decided to lean into it. Wholeheartedly.

I wanted to crawl inside of him. To meld with him, melt into him. I wanted us to become one.

He responded to my kiss with fervent need. His heavy weight pressed me against the wall, the cool bark rough against my shoulder blades. But I was beyond caring, lost as I was in the taste of him. His smoky, honeyed flavor invaded my senses, surrounding me and making my head spin.

The sensations overwhelmed me. His mouth still connected to mine, our tongues engaged in a rhythmic dance as his hands began to roam. They caressed my calf, stroking up and underneath the hem of my nightgown. My leg rose to wrap around his waist, chasing his touch. Those fingers moved higher, brushing against the back of my knee to my thigh. Fabric rose in the wake of his touch until it was over my waist, snagged between me and the wall.

That's when he hitched my other leg around him and took all of my weight into his arms. I was dizzy with longing and barely registered that Keeran was spinning me around and carrying me to the bed. Then my back hit the buttery soft sheets and I sank into the mattress.

He hovered over me, arm muscles bulging on either side of my head. "You want to accept the bond, Niara?" His voice was nectar on gravel, rough and sweet.

I nodded, running my hands up his gloriously bare chest.

"I need to hear you say it. If we do this, then we can never sever the twining—even if the curse is never broken."

His breathing was labored. I could feel how hard he was working to keep himself off of me.

"I accept the bond, Keeran," I said, slowly and clearly. Then wrapped my arms around his neck and pulled him down until he covered me completely.

As we kissed, he somehow managed to remove my nightgown. I tugged at his pants, but he pulled my hands away, trapping both my wrists in one of his own above my head. He loomed there, eyes flashing bright, turning from dark brown to the vibrant fiery flame of the beast. His skin started to glow and behind him, the glimmer of his retracted fire wings danced. I'd never seen them in their fully extended state and hoped they wouldn't set fire to the sheets.

Where our bodies touched, steam rose, heating the room by several degrees. My skin was slippery with sweat. The space between my legs was slick and pulsed with a needy ache. I had never felt so much *want* before.

Keeran's lips seemed to be everywhere at once: my breasts, my belly, my thighs, my knees, my feet, and then back up again. When his mouth traced my ear, his low voice rumbled in unfamiliar words that sparked notes of recognition. It was the language from my dream. Only now, every part of him was very much real and visible to me.

His body slid down mine and stopped, head between my legs, gaze locking me in place. He extended his tongue and took an exploratory lick. I bit my lip to keep from moaning aloud.

As his tongue delved into my folds, I tried to stay quiet, to be mindful of other guests in the inn, but I lost the battle and my cries rose. His tongue was heated as it sunk inside me, lapping at my core until all the buildup within me crested and finally burst.

I was hoarse, my throat suddenly raw as I writhed with the intensity of the pleasure. And then his face was above me. His mouth descended to my own, and I greedily responded, tasting myself on his lips.

His hard length pressed between my legs, begging for entrance. My body was doing its own begging. I needed him, needed him, needed him. And thankfully, he obliged.

He plunged inside of me, causing my back to arch. My lips formed an O as the breath was forced from my body. My eyes widened at the invasion—the feeling of being stretched so far verged on pain.

Heat. There was so much heat on my skin, pouring into me, pouring *through* me from him. It was like we were in this feedback loop sharing our rising temperatures back and forth.

He stroked within me, plunging deeper and deeper, pushing me further, forcing me to take the thick length of him. Whenever I thought I was at capacity, he'd wedge a little more inside me, proving me wrong.

The pleasure was indescribable. A spark of pure bliss ignited within me. Then began to grow. And grow. His powerful thrusts only fanned the flames.

His weight pressed me into the mattress. My legs tightened around his waist, allowing me to take him more fully. My head tipped back. His lips and tongue stroked my neck, jaw, ear. Growling words of praise and pleasure in that language I didn't need to understand to know.

With a shudder, my body seized, reaching another peak. The pleasure went on and on and I vibrated, all tension releasing. Keeran roared, his muscles bulging and turning rigid as he climaxed.

I sucked in breaths, trying to reconnect with my body. Heat still suffused me. Not just between my legs, or on my skin, but deep, deep inside of my chest. I felt like I was in the center of a roaring fire.

And all around us was steam. The entire room was filled with it, as if the bedroom was a sauna at a bathhouse. I wiped the moisture from Keeran's brow and kissed him there.

He fell heavily to my side, taking his weight off of me and exiting my body. And I missed it. I missed the feel of him inside me. I lay there more satisfied than I had ever been in my entire life.

And the spark of something within me that I still couldn't identify was growing and growing.

16

niara

THE AUTOWAGON KEERAN had borrowed from the innkeeper rattled beneath us as we sped along the winding road leading away from the town of Belward. I was piloting. Keeran sat beside me, hunched over, his breathing labored. Each jolt of the vehicle made him wince. Fire danced just beneath the surface of his skin, like tiny lightning storms of orange bursting beneath the deep brown.

"It can't be much farther," I said, casting him worried glances while steering the wagon around the twists in the bumpy road.

The innkeeper had advised us that the Temple of Ignis, located just outside of Belward and along the winding Nyxa River, had been submerged twenty solars ago by a dam built by the Rootborn. That had sparked a bloody conflict between the two Fae groups. After all of the bloodshed and battles, the temple was still underwater, beneath Lake Mynnitunqa, which had since spawned legends of ghostly apparitions seen by visitors.

Pilgrims would travel from far and wide to purify themselves in the waters of Lake Mynnitunqa, which were believed by many to have curative properties.

As the other temples were too far to reach by mid-afternoon, and Keeran was deteriorating rapidly after seeming to rally the day before, we made the decision to head for the lake. For a Water Mage, accessing a submerged temple should be child's play. I fidgeted with the seaglass gem around my neck constantly as the miles passed, hoping I could pull off the relatively simple enchantment.

Overhead, Morros crossed the sky rapidly. The Day Seven eclipse, when both he and Ignis finally caught their beloved sun Lyra for a brief moment, only to have her race off again, was nearly upon us. We had less than half an hour to make it to the temple.

We rounded another bend, and suddenly the lake sprawled before us—vast and glittering under the dual suns. In any other circumstance, I might have found it beautiful. Now, it was just another obstacle.

I brought the autowagon to a stop at the shore. The waters stretched out, deceptively peaceful. Somewhere beneath those depths lay our destination—and Keeran's only chance at breaking the curse.

"How deep is it?" I asked, helping him from the vehicle. He was sweating profusely now, his shirt stuck to his skin.

"One hundred and fifty feet at its deepest point." Dread seeped through our bond. "My cursed form can withstand the water for only short periods of time. And Ember Fae do not swim."

The flames licking through his veins sparked again in several places. He would not be able to keep this shape for much longer.

I knelt at the water's edge, my heart hammering. "What we need is a bubble. Essentially a shell that will let us walk down to the temple protected from both the water and the pressure." The cage that had held Keeran was an example. I couldn't hope to create one with the restrictive properties of the cage, but a simple shell should be easy enough.

"Can you manage that?" Genuine curiosity and not doubt filled his voice.

I nodded, hoping to project more confidence than I felt. "It's a basic water manipulation. All acolytes learn it."

I didn't mention I'd never successfully performed it.

I closed my eyes, clutching the seaglass gem around my neck. Morros's power was distant, but present, and slowly filled the gemstone. I visualized the water before me parting to form a protective dome around us. I pushed my will outward, commanding the lake to bend to my desires.

Nothing happened.

I tried again, focusing harder, sweat beading on my forehead. The water rippled slightly, then settled back into stillness. My cheeks burned with humiliation.

"I just need to—" I reached deeper, channeling everything I had.

A small dome began to form, rising a few inches from the surface—then it collapsed with a splash.

Keeran placed a burning hand on my shoulder. "Niara—"

"I can do this!" I snapped, more at myself than him. I'd never been good enough, had barely mastered the simplest water manipulations. Now, when it mattered most, my failure would cost us everything.

The distant sound of engines made us both turn. On the road behind us, a convoy of vehicles approached, the distinctive blue of Water Mage transports visible even at this distance.

"They've tracked us," I whispered. I'd hoped we'd have more time.

Amal and the wardens had broken the rule about land travel by day during the Holy Convergence. I wondered how he had spun that while keeping his own true reasons for capturing the beast a secret. Maybe the urgency of Keeran's recapture was enough to force the other Archons to give their assent.

Keeran gazed at me, a sad smile bending his lips. "Niara, my love, we are out of time."

keeran

I'd heard the Water Mages approaching from a mile away and had been mentally preparing myself for the battle. Now that they're close, I sense three dozen soldiers. They must have called in reinforcements, because I know they wouldn't have left their high priestess unguarded while they chased me. Hopefully, the strongest wardens are still on the flotilla.

However, that doesn't mean that one against three dozen is going to be easy.

My human form is becoming an impossibility to hold, and so I let it go entirely, transforming into the beast. Since I've been away from the volcano for so many days, I'm far from full strength. But I will do whatever I must in order to protect my mate.

Keep trying, I tell her in my mind, the only way we can communicate when I'm in this form. *I'll hold them off.*

"You can barely stand!"

Then I'll fall fighting.

She nods, tears welling in her eyes, and turns back to the water, kneeling again. Her expression of frustration shreds my heart.

I suspect the reason she's having problems with her water magic is because she's not yet learned to use her fire. I'm not even certain how it would work. Having affinities for both types of magic is unheard of, but this is our only chance. And I'm confident she can do it. I have faith in my mate.

The wardens burst from the tree line, with Amal in the lead. "Move away from the beast, Niara!" he calls, and I let out a roar full of all the fiery anger that has been building for this man over the past week.

How dare he so much as speak my mate's name!

Keep trying, my love, I tell Niara. *I believe in you.*

I pray to Solara for strength. It was the mother sun who breathed life into the volcano to create the Ember Fae. Overhead, she shines mightily, heating the air and the sand. I soak in the warmth and use the small power boost to transform the sand before me into shards of obsidian to block the path of the oncoming attackers.

They toss their magefrost spears at me, but I bat them away easily. Some of the spears fall short of their target and shatter the obsidian barrier. Ignis's power comes to life within me. The Fire Moon is not yet visible in the early afternoon light, but I feel him there in the sky all the same. His power channels through me.

But over the din of battle cries, a female voice is chanting. She is beyond my vision, but I catch snatches of words spoken clumsily in Old Ember, our ancient tongue. This must be the traitorous priestess, the one who wants control of their Order. She is casting a spell to drain me of Ignis's power, and I can feel it starting to take hold.

The attackers reach me, and my mate grows more desperate. She's trying to keep her feelings hidden, but our bond won't allow it. Her fear and shame, disappointment and anger burst within me. I must hold my ground to give her the time she needs to figure this out.

Help my mate, I call out to Ignis mentally. *I cannot lose her when I have only just found her. My family is in disgrace with you, but please have mercy. I have only ever been your servant.*

I pull more from the moon's power and slash out at another opponent, who leaps over the obsidian barrier to try to get me. I will fight as long as I can in order to protect her.

Amal appears behind the wardens, expression grim. Being high warden means a greater level of power and more sophisticated training than the others. He raises a hand and water from the lake streams over me in an arc. It forms a cyclone in midair that descends upon me from above.

The ground assaults, I've been able to parry, but this I cannot. The water hits my skin like razors, and I cry out. Niara's distress blooms within me as the ribbons and blades of water cut into my tough hide

"Keeran!" she screams as I fall to the ground.

17

niara

DESPERATION CLAWED at me as I focused on the lake once more. We had to get to the temple. I had to save him. With shaking hands, I clutched the seaglass gem at my neck and reached out once more to the water, but my commands were still unheeded.

Tears of frustration blurred my vision. Keeran's pain radiated through me, growing more intense with each passing moment. I was failing him, just as I'd failed at every test of my water magic.

As I sank to my knees at the water's edge, a memory surfaced: High Priestess Valya, after my fifth failed trial. She'd found me hiding in the archives, face streaked with tears.

"Perhaps," she'd said thoughtfully, "you fail because you're trying so hard to be what others expect. Stop fighting yourself, Niara. Listen to what the water is telling you."

I'd been so focused on becoming the perfect Water Mage that I'd never truly heard what she was saying. I'd spent my life trying to force myself into a mold created by others, fueled by gratitude and grief.

Behind me, Keeran's roars grew weaker. The cyclone thrashed, and water whips lashed out at him. Our bond held nothing but pain.

Ylena's face contorted in triumph as she continued chanting, using a magic not her own, a magic I didn't even realize Water Mages could wield, to drain Keeran's energy for her own selfish purposes.

I closed my eyes and did something I'd never allowed myself to do before. I stopped struggling. Stopped pushing. Stopped trying to be what the Order wanted me to be.

Instead, I listened.

The quiet was immediate and absolute. The sounds of the ritual, Keeran's pain, the water weapons—all faded away. Within that silence, I sensed two distinct presences. One was cool and fluid, gentle yet unyielding—Morros's embrace, familiar from years of prayer and working to channel his energy. But there was another presence too, one that was hot and vibrant, pulsing with life and energy.

In my mind's eye, I saw them both—Morros, serene and thoughtful, his pale blue form rippling like the surface of a still pool, and beside him, Ignis, blazing with passion and power, his form constantly shifting like living flame. Though Ignis's presence felt new to me, I realized it was not. I had just been trying to suppress that part of me for so long.

The two brother moons were not enemies, as I'd been taught. They were complementary forces, two sides of the same celestial dance.

And they were both reaching for me.

"I see you," Morros whispered. "Child of water."

"I've always known you," Ignis's voice crackled. "Daughter of flame."

I'd been trying to choose between them when I was never meant to choose at all.

Power surged through me, unlike anything I'd ever experienced—cool blue energy from Morros flowing through my left side, and blazing orange heat from Ignis burning through my right. The seaglass gems braided into my hair and the one at my throat simultaneously froze and burned, crackling with conflicting energies that somehow didn't cancel each other out but amplified one another.

Steam rose from my skin, a physical manifestation of the harmony I'd found between these opposing elements. I was not half of one thing and half of another—I was whole, a bridge between water and fire, born to unite what others saw as irreconcilable.

I opened my eyes and confidently lifted my hands toward Lake Mynnitunqa.

"Cease," I commanded, and every water-based weapon disintegrated into droplets and fell harmlessly back into the lake.

"Part," I told the waves, stating it as a simple expression of my desire.

The water obeyed instantly, rolling back from the shore in a thunderous cascade to reveal a wide path leading down into the depths. A staircase made of obsidian was visible in the distance. The water retreated even farther to reveal the small, domed temple made of the black volcanic glass.

I turned back toward the Water Mages and extended my

other hand toward Amal and Ylena. A wall of flame erupted from the ground between us, so hot that the sand beneath it began to melt. The wardens conjured magefrost weapons that hissed and evaporated as they tried to penetrate my fiery barrier.

"No!" Ylena's scream pierced through the roar of the flames. "This isn't possible!"

Amal ordered the wardens to break through, to douse my flames, but their magic was useless. My fire could not be put out by water.

I ran to where Keeran had collapsed, his massive form splayed motionless on the shore. The sand beneath him had already begun to melt from his heat. With a thought, I transformed it fully into glass, creating a smooth surface, then lifted him on a cushion of air.

Niara, he whispered in my mind, his mental voice weak. *How . . .?*

"I stopped fighting who I am," I answered, guiding his floating form toward the path across the lakebed.

Behind us, Ylena continued to scream threats and curses, but her voice grew fainter as we moved along the newly revealed trail. Above, the sky darkened as the dual eclipse began. Ignis appeared as if from nowhere, following Morros as he finally caught Lyra in their perpetual celestial dance.

The temple doors loomed before us, covered in the same elaborate carvings as inside the Obsidian Oculus. They seemed to shimmer with inner light as we approached. The prophecy Keeran had mentioned echoed in my mind: *Where Ignis's power meets Lyra's light, and tempers yield to wisdom's might, devotion true, the curse must prove, with twining vows to his only love.*

I placed my hand against the smooth, dark glass, feeling both fire and water pulse through my veins in perfect harmony.

"We're here," I whispered to Keeran. "And I'm ready to break the curse."

18

niara

ANCIENT FIRE SPARKED in long-dormant torches flanking the entrance, as if recognizing the return of Ignis's son. I gently deposited Keeran at the threshold of the temple. Exhaustion crashed through me like a tidal wave, and I collapsed to my knees beside him. My chest heaved with labored breaths as a torrent of emotions threatened to overwhelm me.

Fear and hope battled within my heart as I looked down at Keeran's immense, dark form. Worry for him consumed me. He was breathing, thank Morros, but he hadn't stirred since we'd left the shore. I pressed my palm against his thick skin, wincing at the heat but unwilling to break contact. The bond between us thrummed with life, reassuring me that he still fought.

With one last concerned glance at him, I summoned my remaining strength and pushed against the ancient door. It swung open with surprising ease, as if it had been waiting for our arrival. I climbed to my feet again and entered.

The interior of the temple stole my breath away. Like the Obsidian Oculus, it was a vast chamber, its walls etched with flowing script that gleamed with an inner fire. But instead of housing a sacred pool, the center of this space was dominated by a great pit that plunged deep into the earth. No water filled this chasm—only darkness that seemed to swallow light itself. I plucked a small pebble from the ground and dropped it into the abyss. No sound returned to mark its landing.

My gaze drifted upward to the ceiling of the temple, where, now that the waters had been pulled back, the structure opened to the sky above. Ignis and Morros were visible, nearly in alignment with Lyra.

Panic and excitement surged through me. We had only moments left.

I rushed back to the entrance where my mate lay motionless. "Keeran!" I called his name, shaking him gently. The rational part of my mind understood he needed rest to heal—most of his wounds had healed over, leaving angry red lines that scored his thick hide—but to break this curse, he needed to awaken.

Inspiration struck. I channeled a stream of water from the lake surrounding us and splashed his face. He groaned and wiped at the liquid with his large, clawed hands. His beast form was terrifying, yes, but also oddly familiar to me now—precious in a way I couldn't have imagined days ago.

Eyes like pools of molten lava snapped open, fixing on me with an intensity that would have once made me shrink away. His mouth—filled with jagged, obsidian teeth—

parted, but no sound emerged. Instead, his voice resonated directly in my mind.

Niara? His mental tone was weak, but alert.

"We're here," I whispered, relief washing through me.

He surveyed our surroundings, and awe transformed his fearsome features. *It's beautiful,* he murmured.

"The eclipse is beginning," I urged, glancing anxiously at the portal above. "We need to start the ritual. What must be done?"

With painful slowness, he rose to his feet, towering above me, and entered the temple. He moved closer to the edge of the pit and peered into its depths, then backed away.

I must make my vows to you, he explained, his mental voice growing stronger. *Do you know what's involved in the twining?*

I nodded slowly, memories of forbidden stories and ancient epic sagas surfacing in my mind. "Only from fairy tales and old poetry. It's . . . beautiful, I've always thought," I said, my cheeks heating at the admission.

He smiled, and what should have been a terrifying expression seemed tender to me. The monstrous face was gentle and affectionate, and my heart swelled in response. He dropped to one knee, his massive form somehow graceful as he extended a clawed hand toward me.

Niara Waterborn, Tidemaiden of the Order of Morros, he began, his voice in my mind rich with emotion. *I vow to share my fire with you, to warm your nights and light your darkest times. I pledge my strength to be your shield, my heart to be your home, and my soul to be forever entwined with yours. Through flame and shadow, I bind myself to you for all eternity.*

I stood transfixed, unsure what response was required.

But just as I started to fidget, some forgotten ancestral memory and knowledge flowed into my consciousness. A combination of vows I'd heard many times at Water Mage ceremonies and those I had never learned yet somehow knew by heart came to mind. Perhaps this was a gift of that Ember Fae ancestor whose blood had given me my fire magic. I spoke the response as if it were being channeled through my very soul.

"Keeran Flameborn, Prince of the Ember Fae, I vow to share my water and fire with you, to warm your nights and cool your days and for us to ever flow as one. I pledge my loyalty to be your protection, my love to be your vessel, and my soul to be forever entwined with yours. Through drought and deluge, ember and ash, I bind myself to you for all eternity."

As the final words left my lips, a deep rumble emanated from the pit, shaking the very foundations of the temple. A golden light began to rise from the depths, growing brighter with each passing moment until it rivaled the glow of the suns themselves. The rumble intensified, and Keeran moved protectively in front of me, shielding me with his massive form.

Above us, through the portal, the celestial dance reached its culmination. Ignis and Morros both slid before Lyra, their combined shadows casting the daughter sun into momentary darkness. For these precious minutes, they would cover her, protecting her from the other moons who eternally sought her favor and from whatever other threats might lurk in the vast expanse of the heavens.

Far away on the coast, High Priestess Valya would be performing the Day Seven ritual—a ceremony that I had studied and practiced for years but had never hoped to master. Now, as I felt the dual powers of water and fire burning within me like twin stars, something profound shifted within my spirit.

The convergence of the celestial bodies—the brother moons both embracing the daughter sun—triggered a transformation deep within my being. It was as if a dam had broken, releasing a torrent of magic that filled every fiber of my existence. The rumbling from the pit grew louder, the light shining brighter, until the entire temple was bathed in a red-gold radiance that seemed to penetrate flesh and stone alike. It washed over Keeran and me, enveloping us in its warm embrace, scouring away all that we had been and revealing what we were meant to become.

When the light finally receded and I blinked my vision clear, my breath caught in my throat. Standing before me was no longer the beast of obsidian and flame, but Keeran in his true Fae form—powerfully built, with skin the color of rich earth and eyes that still held that hint of eternal flame behind their depths. My heart soared at the sight of him restored, his curse shattered by the power of our bond.

Along his hairline, a circlet of golden intertwining curving lines was imprinted on his skin. I raised my hand to it, watching it subtly glow. He brushed his fingers along my forehead as well, and I knew I bore an identical marking. Our twining marks.

My protective barrier, which had kept the lake at bay, began to fracture, allowing water to pour through the high windows of the temple. Yet rather than flooding the sacred space, the water danced midair above the pit, meeting the fire that rose from the depths—the underground volcano upon which this temple had been built so long ago. The elements twisted and twined around each other in an elaborate, breathtaking dance, neither conquering nor yielding, but creating something entirely new in their union.

Moved by instinct and the magic singing in my veins, I raised my hand toward the spectacle. The fire and water responded immediately, shooting upward through the portal to the sky above, creating a pillar of elemental harmony that would be visible for miles.

I turned to Keeran, my eyes brimming with tears of joy, as I threw myself into his arms. His human form—warm and solid—enveloped me in an embrace that felt like coming home after a lifetime of wandering.

"The curse is broken?" I asked, needing to hear the confirmation from his lips.

"Yes," he murmured against my hair, his voice deep and rich. "It's broken. Thank you for freeing me, Niara."

I pulled back just enough to meet his gaze, my hands framing his face. "No, thank you. Now I finally understand my magic. You've freed *me*."

His dark eyes, flecked with embers, searched mine for a moment before he lowered his face to my upturned one. His lips captured mine in a kiss that spoke of promises fulfilled and futures yet to unfold. We remained there, locked in an embrace beneath the light of the dual moons, until they completed their journey past Lyra and continued their eternal chase across the heavens.

epilogue

niara

HAND IN HAND, we made our way back to the lake's shore. My flames had died down, and I wondered why we weren't being greeted by an attack. But the reason soon became clear.

The caravan of Water Mages making their way through the land had not gone unnoticed by the locals. A group of Fireforged Fae had come to investigate. It would have been amusing to watch Amal and Ylena try to talk their way out of an international incident, but Keeran, now curse-free, approached and identified himself as the Prince of Ember-glade, then began negotiations for extradition.

While the wardens under Amal's command had merely been following orders, he and Ylena bore the responsibility and were quickly arrested. The penalty for treason was death in both Ember Fae and Water Mage societies, and

Keeran was going to make sure he was there to enact the final sentence himself.

I asked after Safina and found that she had been imprisoned for helping Keeran escape. It hurt my heart to hear it. The wardens didn't know if she had been sent back to Tidehaven or was still with the flotilla. Finding and freeing my friend was high on my list. But first, Keeran and I had to escort these high-value prisoners back to Ashcrest. And then a tear-filled reunion would no doubt come with his family.

I stood on the lake's shore, peering out at the sparkling waters. Chunks of obsidian and shards of magefrost, which would take months to thaw naturally, littered the sand. The evidence of the conflict here was ugly.

Raising my hand toward the lake, I was able to easily connect with Morros's power now and pushed the waters up and across the beach, causing them to wash the remnants of the battle away. I could feel them floating into the deeper waters, then sinking down to the bottom.

Within my chest, Keeran's satisfaction bloomed. I turned to find him striding toward me. Even dressed in a borrowed cloak and pair of trousers, he looked regal. He smiled, his dark eyes alight with inner fire, and wrapped his arms around me as soon as he was close enough.

"We're going to commandeer the Water Mage vessel and sail home to Ashcrest."

His happiness at going home bled into me, warming me. "You'll get to see your family," I said.

"Yes."

"What do you think they'll think of me?" I tilted my head up, resting it on his chest.

His fingers played with the gems on the ends of my

braids, which had shifted to a color somewhere between blue and purplish black—part seaglass, part obsidian.

"I think that the newest princess of Emberglade will be loved by my family nearly as much as I love her."

My throat clogged, and I blinked back the sudden tears that had filled my eyes.

"You chose me and you saved me," he said, gazing intently into my eyes. "And you accepted the twining, so you aren't going to be able to get rid of me."

"I don't want to," I said, squeezing him tighter. "I love you, Keeran. And I don't want to be anywhere else."

His lips descended toward mine, and I closed my eyes, getting lost in his kiss. I wasn't ready to think about more than this yet. His smoky flavor on my tongue, his strong arms wrapped around me protectively . . . it all made the prospect of being a princess, living among Ember Fae, and learning more about my heritage—plus freeing my best friend—not quite so daunting.

The flame of his presence in my heart grew stronger and stronger. He kissed me until I was breathless, and I knew I had finally found the place where I was meant to be. Keeran was home, and with him, I could always be exactly myself.

download the bonus scene

Don't want the magic to end?

Get an exclusive FREE bonus scene with Niara and Keeran when you join my newsletter!

Head to **https://lpen.co/obsidianbonus** to download it now and stay in the loop on new releases, behind-the-scenes goodies, and special content.

acknowledgments

This series was the brainchild of one of my best friends in the world, Ines Johnson. For those who don't know the story, we met when I was 17 years old, on the campus of Howard University, in the Annenberg Honors Program of the School of Communications.

We lived down the hall from one another freshman year and were roommates in our senior year. After graduation, we both moved away but eventually returned to the DC area and reconnected at a week-long workshop back on Howard's campus.

Our earliest steps toward becoming professional, published authors were also taken together. We read each other's early manuscripts, lost and finally won NaNoWriMo (RIP) together, and self-published our first books within months of each other.

Being a part of the first shared world she was spearheading was an opportunity I just couldn't pass up. I was determined to make the time to write this novella and take part in the world she was building.

As for the story, *The Obsidian Curse* had its early origins in the 1985 film *Ladyhawke*. Fortunately for us all, the story veered wildly from that initial spark. (While the film does not hold up, the overall premise—two star-crossed lovers who can't be human at the same time of day—is still solid.)

I was also inspired, once again, by Cree Summer's 1999 seminal rock album *Street Faërie*. I've had a goal for many years to write a different story based on each track of that album. The two songs "Revelation Sunshine" and "Miss Moon" are the ground from which this book sprouted.

The planet of Lunaterra with its two suns and thirteen moons felt like it fit the basic parameters of the story I'd been brainstorming from those songs.

Bringing a new book into the world is never easy. I want to thank Ines Johnson and all the other authors in Lunaterra for being so amazing to work with.

Thanks to Olivia Bedford, whose feedback is always so on point and insightful. To my copyeditor Sydnee Thompson, who whips my punctuation into shape. (She didn't edit this note, so all errant commas are mine.) To Lisa Vincent for all of her help and support. Thanks to narrators Caroline Sorunke and Pierre Manhattan for bringing the audiobook to life.

Thanks to Dominick for walking away in the middle of our first conversation, LOL. To my brother Paul for reading another one of my kissing books, even though it's not his thing, and still managing to give me good feedback. And to my mom, who gave me the writing gene.

To all my readers, y'all are the reason why I get to do this. I can't ever thank you enough for reading. ♡

about the author

L. Penelope has been writing since she could hold a pen and loves getting lost in the worlds in her head. She is an award-winning fantasy and paranormal romance author. Her novel *Song of Blood & Stone* was chosen as one of *TIME* Magazine's 100 Best Fantasy Books of All Time. Equally left and right-brained, she studied filmmaking and computer science in college and sometimes dreams in HTML. She hosts the *My Imaginary Friends* podcast, co-hosts the *Ink and Magic* podcast, and lives in Maryland with her feline dependents.

www.lpenelope.com
hello@lpenelope.com